Home For Christmas

CANDEE FICK

DEDICATION

To all my faithful readers
who begged to know what happened next...
I listened.
And this book's for you..

CHAPTER ONE

On a Monday afternoon in mid-October, Tyler Sherwood found himself pacing backstage at the Showstopper Theater inside the Golden Palace Casino in Las Vegas. Nervous energy pulsed through his veins.

Three hours to showtime. And as one of the seven remaining groups still competing in *Making Music*, tonight's performance was another step toward a recording contract and nationwide attention.

Of course, the nation didn't know about him—them—yet. After all, the weekly episodes featuring the good and bad auditions had only just begun to be broadcast. Not to mention, tonight's concert in front of yet another half-drunk audience sworn to secrecy wouldn't air for another month and a half...

But it *would* air.

And viewers would once again get to hear the tight harmonies the judges had raved about while enjoying their mash-up medleys of bygone hits. Compilations that he had arranged just like he had originally recruited the members of their group to perform on a stage in Branson, Missouri.

With his brother. At his family's theater.

But still, the group had been his dream from the beginning.

And now that the dream was within grasp, he should be upstairs resting in the suite he shared with the other men. Staying hydrated. Or even blocking out choreography for the new medley they'd started rehearsing with the girls that morning under the direction of their assigned coach.

But something about the gleam in the man's eyes and his extensive professional connections told Tyler that things were about to change for the better.

His big break was just around the corner.

A familiar high-pitched giggle echoed along the concrete corridors. He cringed at the chalkboard-scratching-equivalent sound. Brittany's ambition to succeed matched his own, but really, why couldn't she tone it down?

Tyler headed in the direction of the noise. At least the distraction of flirting with the beautiful woman would help pass the hours until call time. However, as he neared the open door to the green room, he heard the rumble of a deeper—decidedly male—voice and slowed.

"Are you sure he won't mind?"

Another irritating giggle trickled out of the room. "He was just a means to an end."

Tyler stopped in his tracks. Who? A weight pressed on his chest. That didn't sound good.

"If you say so." This close, the man's voice was eerily familiar. "Should I feel bad that your group is getting cut tonight?"

Cut? Even worse. And yet how could that be true? The judge's scores weren't collected after each act performed and the final tally to determine which groups would continue in the contest was not announced until the conclusion of the evening's concert.

Unless there was a secret script somewhere, who could possibly know the fate of the individual acts hours before they took the stage?

"I don't like losing, but…" Brittany made a purring noise. "In this case, it gives me the chance to spend more time with you."

The distinctive sound of kissing filled the silence.

Surely she wasn't cheating on him?

The knot in his stomach tightened but he had to know the truth. To see it with his own eyes.

Tyler risked a peek into the room and quickly pulled back, his vision seared with the image of their coach—also one of the judges—with his arms wrapped around and lips passionately locked with Tyler's girlfriend.

Or at least he'd assumed that's what Brittany was. Had been.

Except in the marathon of rehearsals starting back in Missouri and culminating here in Las Vegas, had they ever made their relationship status official? Had he even wanted to?

No. He'd soaked up her flattery and affection but kept his options open. And in the process of feeding his ego, walked right into her trap. He'd pursued fickle fame and turned his back on his family all because of a woman who thought of him only as the means to an end. Who had used him to punch her ticket to Vegas.

And now he had nothing. No girlfriend. No trust. No true friends in town. And if the outcome of tonight's show was fixed, apparently soon no stage to perform on.

I've been a fool.

He knocked his head back against the cement blocks. Now what?

"You can move into my suite tonight and tomorrow I'll introduce you to your new backup singers. Baby, it's time to officially forget about that has-been with his out-of-date songs."

Tyler winced, then pushed away from the wall to retreat back the direction he'd come.

"Just watch. I'm going to make you a star."

Brittany's answering squeal was almost as irritating as her laugh.

A star.

While his star had just burned out.

And after tonight's performance aired, the whole nation would see his humiliation.

CHAPTER TWO

Grace Mitchell deposited an armload of dirty plates and coffee cups into the plastic tub near the kitchen door, then picked up a soapy rag. Another Friday morning at the Way Stop and the breakfast rush was over. If one could call a dozen diners a rush.

After wiping down the few tables where they—she—served a limited menu of breakfast and lunch options, her gaze roamed past the small grocery area to the far wall where her dad was busy cleaning up behind the bait and boat rental counter.

Complete with rustic Missouri decor, their Ed Stilley guitar on the wall, and country music on the radio, the Way Stop was home.

And with the stream of locals and seasonal influx of tourists flocking to the shores of Table Rock Lake, there would always be a need for such a business. Always be a need for her.

Grace sighed and turned to start another batch of coffee. The locals loved their brew with every meal.

A minute later, the background music changed. To a very familiar song.

Grace whirled to see her dad standing beside their stereo system. "What did you do that for?"

He shrugged. "I like hearing you sing." But there was a twinkle in his eyes like he was up to something.

Her fingers twitched as if eager to play along with the melody, but she grabbed her rag again to clean the nearby counter.

Dad chuckled. "Don't hate me, but I like knowing that a part of you and your music will always stay here even when you don't."

"Am I going anywhere?"

"You should." His expression shifted. They'd had this conversation multiple times since she'd graduated from college back in May.

But even as she turned away and gripped the edge of the drink station with whitening knuckles, the background music seeped into her conscience. It actually didn't sound half bad considering her amateur equipment.

What would it sound like with Nashville's touch?

No. That dream was just a dream. Her life was here now, in rural Ridgedale. And the sooner Dad accepted that, the better.

She turned once again to face him. "I told you what the principal said. When Mrs. Hartford retires, the job's as good as mine."

"You really want to spend your days corralling elementary and middle school students and trying to get them to sing in harmony when they'd rather be anywhere else?" He raised his eyebrows.

Grace hid her wince at the accurate description of what she'd discovered during her student teaching and forced a smile. "It's what I went to college for." And the years away from home had been difficult, especially after her widowed father had suffered a mild heart attack her junior year.

"You might have graduated with a teaching degree, but I still don't understand why you switched majors. Or why you won't pursue this." He waved a hand at the disc player with the music she'd created for a class project back when her plan had been a degree in music performance with a minor in recording arts.

That project that had reignited her creativity and dreams and a flurry of new music…until she'd caught an episode of *American Idol* and retreated to reality. She'd never be good enough and she was better off pursuing a stable career instead of the stage. Even if switching direction mid-stream cost her two additional years of working to pay her way through college. She might technically have a double major with an additional minor to her name, but only planned to use one of her degrees.

She cleared her throat. "What's so wrong with it? Why can't I be a teacher like you?" She stepped closer and nodded toward his left. To the corner where a few of his handcrafted instruments were on display and a door led to the small studio where he offered private lessons in the winter months.

Dad grunted.

"It's true." She tightened the elastic band on her pony tail. "However, until a full-time job opens up, I could always take over some of your students and give you more time in your workshop." And that full-time job might take a while to materialize since she hadn't applied anywhere outside the Branson and Hollister area, but unless she wanted to move further away from home, her options were limited.

Her stomach balked against the feeling that she was bogged down in a muddy rut like those outside after the rains. But she didn't know how to break free from the routine.

Music was like the beating of her heart, except…

Dad sighed. "Gracie, I know you want to be around to take care of your old man, but not at the expense of the gifts God gave you. You don't truly belong here." She couldn't ignore the pleading in his eyes.

"But I—"

"If you won't leave the nest on your own, to mount up on wings like eagles…"

Her heart caught in her throat. Nothing quite like the squeeze between longing for more and the fear of falling. But life was safe here where she knew what to expect. Where every day and every season had its own rhythm.

Dad narrowed his eyes. "I've decided to give you a push."

"A what?" She glanced around the empty room. Oh, where were the customers when she needed them?

"A nudge. A test. A dipping of your toes in the water."

"Stop with the stalling. What did you do?"

Dad tilted his head toward the stereo. "I sent your demo tape to a friend and he's passing it on to a friend of his in Nashville."

"But..." It wasn't Dad's place to do that without her permission. And yet, what would they think?

Grace collapsed onto a chair and folded her arms over her Mitchell's Way Stop *We feed all the critters* T-shirt, trying in vain to contain the squirming, flailing, flopping of her insides.

"At least then you'll know."

Tears flooded her eyes. "Know what?" That she wasn't good enough? That she was truly stuck in a classroom trying to inspire kids to care about her passion?

"You'll never know if God has a different plan for your life unless you knock on a few doors."

She caught her breath. "If that door opens..." She'd have her dream of creating music but would also have to step onto a stage. Into a world of always performing. A world that might change her into someone she didn't want to become.

She'd seen it happen to others and wasn't strong enough to face it herself.

At least not today.

She stood and retreated toward the tub of dirty dishes that needed washing.

"You can't run from this forever, Gracie. Will you at least pray about it?"

She looked back to see the concern on his face and her shoulders slumped. "I can do that."

But only that.

CHAPTER THREE

A week after getting officially cut from *Making Music*, Tyler pulled his rental car out of the lot at the small Branson airport.

Where should he go?

He turned north toward Hollister. Toward home. His former home.

Yet what kind of welcome could he expect after leaving the way he had? After all, he'd been the one to cut the ties. Let his apartment lease go and put most of his belongings— including his pickup truck—in storage before heading off to Las Vegas to chase a foolish dream.

His brother might have picked him up at the airport. Might even help him retrieve his own wheels and return the rental. Give him a couch to crash on.

Except no one knew he was coming back, mostly because he was too embarrassed to admit his mistakes. Too much time had passed for an easy apology, but the sharp memories of those last conversations with his family—and his twin— haunted him.

And what could he say now to undo the damage?

Tyler let off the accelerator, then pulled into a gas station. Yes, he was stalling. Because he certainly didn't need fuel but maybe grabbing a bite of food would be smart. Everyone needed to eat and he could use another moment to shake off the past and come up with a plan.

But before he could get out of the car, his phone chimed with a reminder. Mom's birthday was today. The date had been the furthest thing on his mind when he'd booked his ticket, but after being reminded of her special day, should he call or just show up on her doorstep with a bouquet of flowers?

His gut clenched. He wasn't ready to face her. It might be better to test the waters of his reception first. Before he could talk himself out of it, he dialed her number.

She answered on the second ring. "Tyler? Is that really you?"

Moisture flooded his eyes and blurred his vision. Digging deep for courage, he forced cheer into his voice. "It's me. Just wanted to wish you a Happy Birthday."

"Oh, thank you. I didn't think you'd remember."

Tyler winced. "No way would I forget something like that." Especially with the date programmed into his phone, but he had no reason to tell her that.

"I can't wait to tell the others tonight." Her soft laugh warmed his heart and tugged him toward home. "They'll never believe that their famous brother took time away from his television show to call, especially since you couldn't make it home for Robin's wedding."

He squeezed his eyes shut. How had he missed being there for his little sister's special day? Was he that self-absorbed?

As if the mention of one sibling opened the gates, his mom spent the next several minutes catching him up on the rest of the family news. Matt and Mary were expecting their third child while his sister Joy and her husband were expecting their first. Nick was engaged to Gloria and planning a Valentine's wedding. Little John was still dating his high school sweetheart and had started college while Gavin had met a girl online. A real sweetheart who worked in Springfield but they were all hoping she'd move to Branson soon.

"And you're in Vegas."

Tyler flinched, then gazed out the car window at the rolling hills of southern Missouri. The time had come to tell her the truth. He opened his mouth…

"The best gift of all is knowing that all of my kids' dreams are coming true."

He swallowed his confession. No. His dreams lay shattered in a casino several states away.

"Thanks again for calling. You made my day. I love you, son."

"I love you, too." Tyler choked out the words before ending the call.

Why hadn't he told her he was back in the area? And what kind of coward did that make him?

He caught a glimpse of himself in the rearview mirror.

Who was that man? There was no sparkle in his eyes. No joy.

No, he'd left that back in Vegas after pretending he hadn't gambled his future in music with a longshot psuedo-reality television show. Pretending it didn't matter and that he could simply return home and pick up the pieces of his former life.

Except with all of his siblings living their dreams, he couldn't show up in defeat with his tail between his legs. A failure. A shell of the man he used to be.

He might be only miles from home, but inside—where it mattered—he was still states away. Where did he go wrong?

Ugh. Too much introspection.

Tyler yanked open the door, then slammed it shut behind him.

Once inside the gas station, he headed straight for the coolers of bottled drinks and the small selection of ready-made sandwiches.

While deciding if he wanted a bag of chips or a candy bar to complete his lunch, someone clapped him on the shoulder.

"Gavin, my man."

Tyler pasted a smile on his face and turned to face a complete stranger. It wasn't the first time someone mistook him for his brother, but after working so hard to be the twin who everyone noticed first, the mistaken identity stung. "Hey." He searched his memories for a name to attach to the somewhat familiar face but came up empty.

"What brings you this far south?" Obviously the man hadn't figured out his error, leaving Tyler to either enlighten him…or pretend.

Tyler held up his food. "Just taking a drive and needed a snack before I head back home." Wherever that was.

"Well, had fun meeting Sally. Say hello when you see her next, will you?"

As if he knew a Sally. Must be Gavin's new girl.

Too late to correct the mistake now. Tyler nodded. "Will do."

"You're a lucky man." Another clap on the shoulder and the stranger moved off toward the register.

Lucky? Not so much anymore.

Between getting cut from the show, his mother's news report, and now a stranger's confusing him with his brother, the blows to Tyler's ego just kept on hitting. He found himself acting and smiling on the outside, but desperately raw and disillusioned and empty on the inside.

He'd become a shallow performer instead of a man of substance. Hadn't been raised that way…

But one thing was certain, he needed to stay away from the other Sherwoods until he could figure it out. Until he could return home with a plan…and maybe even a girl on his arm.

But where could he hide?

As he grabbed a bag of chips to round out his meal, he overheard two other customers near the soda fountain talking about switching gears from fishing to hunting.

Good old Missouri outdoorsmen.

Wait. Fishing. Table Rock Lake.

His great uncle Joshua had a cabin not far away that was always open for the family to use. But in late October with fishing season over for the year, chances were it was unoccupied and just waiting for him.

Tyler detoured down another aisle to add a few cans of ready-to-eat soup to his armload, then snagged a baseball cap and a pair of sunglasses from another display for a disguise before checking out.

Once back in his rental car, he turned south and soon took the exit for Ridgedale. A mile west of the small town, he spotted a billboard-type sign for Mitchell's Way Stop.

"Breakfast, Bait, Boats, and More." He chuckled. As if anyone would want to eat breakfast at a location that also sold bait.

Still the location wasn't too far from his destination.

A neon "Open" sign in the window beckoned and he turned into the gravel parking lot. Might as well check out what they had to offer. Because if he could eat a few meals here and restock his supplies, he wouldn't have to drive back into town for groceries and risk being recognized.

He snorted. Already thinking like a hermit...

With tennis shoes crunching across the rocks, he approached the entrance.

Where a woodburned sign above the door read "We feed all the critters."

Welcome back to the Missouri Ozarks.

CHAPTER FOUR

Grace cringed at the sour notes filtering through the closed door to her dad's studio. How long would it take for little Blake to remember how to tune his guitar?

However, Dad had more than enough patience, especially when it came to the parade of beginner students referred by the local homeschooling co-op.

And she—the one planning to make a career out of teaching—couldn't bear to be in the same building. Something was horribly wrong with that picture and the uncomfortable realization she might have wasted several years of her life pursuing a path she never wished to walk.

Grace turned up the radio to drown out her thoughts and the discordant sound next door, then grabbed a rag and scrubbed at the already clean tables.

The clanging bell on the main door announced the arrival of a tall man who removed his sunglasses before looking around.

Tyler Sherwood.

She recognized him instantly despite the baseball cap covering most of his dark brown hair. As handsome as ever with broad shoulders stretching the fabric of his long-sleeved thermal above equally solid jean-clad legs. Her traitorous heart skipped a couple beats as if it had forgotten all about her high school heartbreak.

Then again the man could be his brother.

No. Her pulse had only ever done that around a certain one of the twins.

His lips curled into a smirk as he eyed the bait and boat rental counter, then he turned toward the corner of empty tables.

She straightened before he caught her staring. "Welcome to the Way Stop." That was professional, right? Casual? But would he recognize her?

His gaze skipped over her, then focused on the shelves of canned goods.

Disappointment stabbed. But what did she expect when caught wearing a ratty T-shirt and her ponytail sticking out the back of her own ball cap?

A true smile crossed his face. Apparently he was more pleased at the sight of peanut butter, applesauce, and soup than another human.

She cleared her throat. "Can I help you find anything in particular?"

His focus shifted from the crowded shelves to the empty restaurant's posted menu, and finally back to her. "Just checking out the…merchandise." His eyes swept up and down while his grin grew. He stepped closer. "And I like what I see."

Grace resisted the urge to cross her arms over her chest as two thoughts slammed into her brain. First, the outrageous flirt was definitely Tyler. And second, he had changed. Become rougher. More worldly.

"Maybe you can show me around later?" A raised eyebrow and Elvis lip curl were proof he craved her attention. Or any attention.

Her stomach churned. If this was what fame did to a person, no thanks. This version of Tyler was a far cry from the boy she used to have a crush on.

She retreated around the end of the counter. "Not interested in giving any tours."

His eyes widened as if surprised at her response.

She bit her lip to hide her laugh. "But if you're hungry, today's special is a Reuben sandwich with chips."

He shook his head, then leaned across the counter. "Already ate. But maybe I can change your mind." Even with those striking eyes and deliberately husky voice, his second attempt at a flirtation was just as pathetically false as the first.

Grace tossed her cleaning rag into the bucket of soapy water and braced her hands on the wooden surface. "That tired line isn't going to work on me. So, what brings you to this neck of the woods?"

*****

What brought him to this neck of the woods? Utter humiliation.

And getting rejected by the cute girl with the *Gone Fishin'* T-shirt wasn't helping matters any.

Except, even though the show was over, he had to keep faking it somehow.

Tyler cleared his throat. "I'm staying up the road for a few days." Or more. "Just checking to see what you've got in stock to save me a trip back to town."

"Up the road, you say?" She quirked an eyebrow over the most unique shade of green eyes he'd seen in years. Almost reminded him of— "There are only a few cabins up that way."

"Maybe I'm on the wrong road." Not really, but he couldn't let her connect the dots if he stood any chance of remaining anonymous for a few days. Time to change the subject... "Oh, I didn't catch your name."

"Didn't catch yours either." A teasing glint sparked in her amazing eyes, almost like she was laughing at him.

He shifted on his feet. "I'm Ty... Wood." He offered his best smile and an extra eyebrow waggle to cover the verbal hesitation.

She smirked. "Nice to meet you. *Ty*. I'm Grace Mitchell." Like the sign out front.

She paused as if waiting for his reaction. Except he was totally out of his element and the whole encounter was going downhill fast. The practiced moves that usually earned the admiration of countless women in the audience were actually turning her off... Making him the object of her scorn if her eye roll was to be believed.

Granny would say it was time for him to be himself, but he didn't know who that was anymore. And he wouldn't figure it out standing here.

Tyler pushed away from the counter and stalked over to the shelves. He grabbed a loaf of bread, peanut butter, coffee, and a few more cans of soup. That should be enough to tide him over for a few days.

He dumped the food on the counter and waited for Grace to ring up his total. Except when he pulled out his wallet to pay, he hesitated. If he handed her his credit card, his lie, er, selective editing of his name would be revealed.

He bypassed the card and reached for cash instead.

However, if he was going to stay around the area for a few days without people discovering his identity, he would need more than a hat, sunglasses, and a false name. Maybe a beard? After all, that disguise seemed to work for his younger brother Nick.

A minute later, he carried the plastic bag of groceries to the car and continued on down the road. About a quarter mile later, he almost missed the turn down the dirt road but soon spotted the small cabin.

After parking behind the structure where curious neighbors—like Grace—wouldn't readily see his car, he wandered toward the lake. As he took in the view of the water through the trees, he could almost feel the stress of the past months rolling off his shoulders.

If they had a few warmer days, he might enjoy sitting on the end of the dock and tossing a line in the water for old time's sake.

A breeze rustled the yellowed leaves overhead and sent a chill down his spine.

But that wouldn't be today.

He turned toward the rental car and started unloading. A few trips later, he had his suitcases stowed beside the quilt-covered bed and his groceries arranged on the open shelves above the old gas range.

Thankfully, there was running water—once he'd turned back on the valves—and basic plumbing instead of an outhouse plus electricity enough to power a few lamps and a tiny dormitory refrigerator. But no heat other than a fireplace. No television. No internet except on his phone…and that had spotty cell service out here in the middle of the woods.

How long could he stand being here?

How long before he craved home cooking like Mom's? Then again, he'd also have to face her all-knowing eyes that would pierce the shell around his heart. And dad's disappointed look.

Nope. Not going there until he had to even if it meant he finding an ax and chopping a pile of wood so he didn't freeze.

As the sun sank low in the sky, he opened a can of soup and dumped it into a dented pan that had seen better days.

Just like him.

CHAPTER FIVE

"Mercy, I'm so glad you stopped by this afternoon."
Grace stirred the pot of homemade spaghetti sauce,
then glanced at the little boy placing napkins beside each plate
with the help of his mother. "And that you brought Jake. He's
growing gangbusters."

Her twin rolled her eyes. "You and your backwoods
phrases."

"Better than comparing him to a weed." Grace resisted
the urge to stick out her tongue. Barely.

"Whatever." Mercy patted her son on the head. "Why
don't you go tell Grandpa that dinner's almost ready?"

The dark-headed boy scurried down the hall while Mercy
moved to the counter to chop a tomato for the salad. As they
worked together to finish preparing the meal, a lump grew in
Grace's throat at the glimpse of the family they used to be.
Before Mom died. Before Mercy…

Before Mercy needed mercy. But then again, didn't they
all?

Soon, Jake and Dad were back and the kitchen rang with
laughter as they gathered around the table and loaded their
plates with spaghetti.

"So, Mercy-girl…" Dad waved a piece of garlic bread in
his daughter's direction. "How's school going for you?"

"Seems I've heard that question before while sitting at this table." Mercy rolled her eyes, then giggled. "But actually, I'm almost done with the cosmetology program."

Grace took a bite of salad and took a closer look at her sister's chin-length hair. The honey-blonde color they shared as identical twins was now hidden beneath an abundance of purple highlights. Or were those auburn?

"It only took me six years to complete a six-month program." Mercy's self-deprecating laugh didn't tell the whole story. Her life had taken a left turn when her high school rebellion continued to steer her off track in college.

Grace wrapped an arm around her sister's shoulders and squeezed. "But you finally found something you love to do. So, now what? A job in Little Rock?"

Mercy shrugged. "I enjoy working with clients, but one of our last units involved a few business classes and I'd like to learn more. I'm seriously considering taking a few online classes through the U of A at night once I get a job." She shifted her gaze to her plate. "Actually, that's one reason I made the trip today. I had an interview at a new salon in Ridgedale."

Was her sister really thinking to move back home?

Grace's squeal was echoed by Dad's whoop and punctuated by an awkward group hug over the table top.

"Grandpa? You got s'ketti sauce on your shirt." Jake's innocent voice broke into their emotional reunion.

"Thanks, buddy." Dad sat down and swiped at the spot with his napkin.

Mercy cleared her throat. "It sounded like a bit of a long shot but there are several other places in Branson I could try as well." She turned her attention to their dad. "But I wondered if Jake and I could stay here for a while. I'd be more than happy to help out at the Way Stop in exchange for—"

"Hush. Of course you're welcome here." He chuckled. "Guess Mercy and Grace really are following me all the days of my life."

Grace groaned. Why Mom had ever agreed to name them the Biblical match set was still a mystery.

Their conversation soon turned to the logistics of her sister moving back at Thanksgiving since it could take a month for her to finish her classes, give her notice at work, and pack up their apartment. It would be nice to reconnect with this new—responsible—version of Mercy instead of the one who always needed to be the center of attention.

Her mind jumped back to earlier in the day and her unexpected customer. Perhaps the need for attention was part of Tyler's problem.

Dad tapped the table with his knuckles. "Actually, your moving home is perfect timing."

"Really?" Mercy seemed more curious than concerned as she helped herself to another plate of spaghetti.

He darted a glance Grace's direction. "I have a feeling Gracie will be moving on soon. I sent her demo tape to a friend in Nashville on Friday."

Her stomach churned at the reminder, but unlike back in high school, Mercy grinned. "That's awesome!"

Grace searched her sister's face but found no hint of jealousy at all. "Don't get too excited. I'm not sure it will go anywhere."

Mercy smiled even wider. "Even if you're not a performer, they might want to buy the rights to your songs."

"Hmm. Hadn't thought about that." And she should have. But could she handle hearing another artist sing her songs when the lyrics had poured from her own heart? Probably not, even for a paycheck.

"But..." Mercy nudged their father with her elbow. "I happen to agree with Dad. You'd be like a new Taylor Swift but with Christian lyrics."

She gasped. The star had started in the industry at a very young age and risen to fame very quickly. Grace couldn't imagine the pressure.

"Although you'd have to ditch the ball caps and jeans to look the part."

Grace eyed her *Gone Fishin'* T-shirt, as if her wardrobe was her biggest obstacle. "You mean this wouldn't fit in Nashville?"

Mercy tilted her head. "Actually, it might. Except not on stage. Speaking of which, you should get used to wearing some makeup now. I know that stage makeup gets laid on pretty thick."

Stage makeup? "But I won't—"

Her arguments were overwhelmed by her sister's enthusiasm and before dessert was served, Grace had been talked into letting Mercy cut her hair into a sleek shoulder-length bob like her own—without the colored highlights—and they'd made plans to drive to the drugstore in nearby Hollister for the basics to accent her green eyes.

The whole makeover conversation seemed like a shove into the deep end of fashion, and yet she couldn't refuse the expression on Dad's face as he listened to his girls. If a haircut and a little mascara was all it took to make him happy, she'd go along.

For now.

But as she loaded their dishes into the dishwasher, she couldn't help but wonder what Mr. Flirty Sherwood would think of her new look. Not that he'd ever see it. Because even if he really was staying somewhere nearby, chances of him visiting the Way Stop again were slim to none.

Just like her chances of getting a record deal.

***

Two days after his first visit, Tyler pulled his truck into the parking lot at Mitchell's Way Stop.

His pulse still thundered with adrenaline after the near miss.

In a town the size of Branson, who would have thought it would be so complicated to avoid the members of his extended family? After dropping off the rental car at the airport, he had grabbed a free shuttle to a hotel in Branson, then called a taxi to drop him off near the storage facility so he could retrieve his own vehicle and several boxes of warmer clothes.

But not only had he spotted—and avoided—one uncle at the first gas station he'd pulled into and then an aunt coming out of the bank where he'd detoured by the ATM for more cash, one of his cousins had been stopped next to him at the light. Tyler had avoided any eye contact and made a quick turn south out of town.

And completely forgot to stop at a grocery store along the way.

He slapped the steering wheel. Since he didn't think he was lucky enough to avoid detection a fourth time, there were more peanut butter sandwiches and soup on the horizon.

After quick-stepping through the drizzle, he ducked through the door and made his way to the shelves where he loaded up with another supply of easy-to-fix staples and set them on the counter near the register.

"I'll be with you in a minute."

He turned at the somewhat familiar voice to see Grace waiting on a couple seated near the window. Except he almost didn't recognize her without the baseball cap. And was her hair shorter or something?

He shifted on his feet, very aware of the limited bathing options at the cabin and the lack of laundry facilities. A subtle dip of his nose toward his shoulder confirmed his suspicions. After all the wood chopping and running around that morning, he was definitely not in a position to impress the lady.

And why did he want to?

Seeking a distraction, Tyler browsed the shelves again and added a few more items to his pile, including a bag of tiny chocolate bars.

"Sorry about the wait." Up close, he was once again captivated by her eyes. Was she wearing makeup or was he more aware since the brim of her former cap wasn't shading them today?

He grunted and tried to avoid staring as she rang up and bagged his purchases. But there was something about her that kept drawing his attention.

Get a grip, Tyler.

He glanced around the rest of the establishment instead. While he'd noticed the bait and boats options during his first visit, this time he was more aware of the few instruments hanging on the wall near a side door.

One of the guitars resembled a battered, odd-shaped mess. And were those words on it? He squinted. *True Light. True Faith. Have Faith in God.*

It was like a personal message.

"If you're getting ready for trick-or-treaters, we don't get many out this way."

"What?" He turned back to where Grace held up his chocolate stash. "No, those are just for me."

A small smile curved her lips. "I like your style." She waved a hand toward the shelves. "Although they're even better with marshmallows and graham crackers."

His eyes widened. "S'mores." And his stomach growled. "I'll be right back."

Her chuckle warmed his heart as he scoured the shelves for the additional items.

Too soon, he'd handed over more of his cash and picked up the bags. With a nod, he turned toward the exit.

And paused briefly for one last glance at the strange guitar. *True Light. True Faith. Have Faith in God.*

Was that what he'd been missing lately? His faith in God?

Once back at the cabin, he quickly put away the food and started a fire. Then dusted off the contemporary version of the Bible he'd found on the bookshelf under the window.

He couldn't even remember the last time he'd read his own Bible—or where it was—let alone attended a church service. No wonder he'd gotten blinded by the stage lights.

True Light. True Faith. Have Faith in God.

Time to take those first steps back.

After taking a seat near the fireplace, he opened the book somewhere in the middle. Jeremiah. The weeping prophet, right? But before he could turn the page to something more encouraging like Psalms, his eyes were drawn to an underlined passage.

"This is God's Word on the subject: 'As soon as Babylon's seventy years are up and not a day before, I'll show up and take care of you as I promised and bring you back home."

His heart skipped a beat. Would God really bring him back home? And how?

"I know what I'm doing. I have it all planned out. Plans to take care of you, not abandon you, plans to give you the future you hope for."

Could it be true? Pressure and longing grew in his chest.

"When you call on me, when you come and pray to me, I'll listen."

The promise wrapped itself around his heart and Tyler slid to his knees on the rough, wooden floor. "Oh, God. I'm so sorry. Please forgive me." Tears flowed along with the regret-laden memories.

But as the truth explored his soul and brought his mistakes into the light, Tyler knew that every confessed sin was forgiven. And still he emptied himself of all the pride and arrogance as well as the false belief that he could be the master of his own life and chart his own course.

As the healing began, other scriptures from his youth and time spent with Granny flooded his mind. He reached once more for the abandoned book and flipped the pages to other highlighted sections.

Thoughts of food and the uncomfortable floor fell by the wayside as he read until it was too dark to see the pages. By the time he collapsed onto the lumpy mattress and pulled the quilt over his shoulders, his heart felt lighter than it had in years.

The prodigal son had seen the light and come home to true faith.

CANDEE FICK

CHAPTER SIX

Saturday morning found Grace running the Way Stop by herself and pouring coffee for the few locals still gathered to debate and solve the world's problems. Just like every Saturday.

Except with the slower winter months and reduced hours of operation starting on Monday, there wasn't enough work to keep her busy. And if Dad hadn't retreated to his workshop to get a jump start on the Christmas orders, there would be two of them standing around doing little to nothing.

She replaced the half-full pot on the warmer and leaned against the drink counter.

Would Dad still need her help once Mercy returned? Would she be demoted to babysitting her nephew? Or was God preparing the way for her to get that teaching job after all?

The clang of the bell interrupted her dreary thoughts. Finally, a customer to serve.

And not just anyone, but Tyler. Her heart skipped a beat.

His eyes swept over her new look and a slight smile curved his lips, but like Thursday when he'd loaded up on ingredients for s'mores, he didn't flirt.

Perhaps that was because of the presence of other customers, but she found herself equal parts disappointed and confused at his change in behavior. Why was she getting so worked up over something so trivial? Was she that desperate for a compliment?

She fingered the shorter strands of her hair. Personally, she liked the change. And while she couldn't wear her hair in a ponytail anymore, she'd found the new style equally easy to maintain since she could always clip the top back into a barrette and let the sides hang down.

After a quick visual sweep of the room, Tyler avoided a return trip to the semi-bare grocery shelves and instead slid into an empty chair at a table near the window.

Well, that was new.

She headed his direction. "What can I get for you?"

He eyed the other customers who appeared to be wrapping up their latest debate. "Coffee, please. To start."

"Sure." She retreated to fetch a clean cup and the pot, then returned.

He nodded his thanks and reached for the cream and sugar packets already on the table.

With a loud scraping noise, a few of her regulars scooted back their chairs to leave and she hurried to meet them at the register. But even as she was settling their bills and chatting about the changing seasons, her eyes kept flitting to the window and the handsome, if scruffy, man sipping coffee with slumped shoulders as if deep in thought.

What was different about him? Besides the growing beard…

And why did she care? She would only risk more pain by investing time or energy wondering about the man. It didn't matter what brought him here because as soon as whatever issue was resolved, he would move on.

Except despite wanting to protect her heart, there was something new in his eyes today. Something genuine and real and broken. Humility looked good on him.

No, she was only imagining things.

But as she busied herself clearing the dirty cups from the previously occupied tables, like a magnet, her mind kept drifting back to the table by the window.

The Tyler she used to know would never be content to linger over coffee in a backwoods cafe.

Would he ever be interested in a girl from Ridgedale? No, he belonged on the stage surrounded by fans.

In the spotlight.

The last place she ever wanted to be. Maybe.

Once the bell clanged behind the last customer, Grace crossed the room and scrambled for a topic. "Can I get you a sandwich or something, Tyler?"

He jolted in his seat. "My name is—"

"Ty...ler Sherwood."

"How did you know?" He frowned.

"Remember the first day you walked in here?" She propped a hand on her hip. "I'd recognize that lip-quirking Elvis impersonation move anywhere."

Was that a blush creeping up his cheeks?

"And here I thought I was being anonymous while all along you knew." He shook his head. "You must have been to concert or two."

She swallowed hard against the memory. "Only one. At a church camp back in high school." But she'd watched him every day in the halls at school for months before that.

He raised an eyebrow and pointed to the chair across from him. "Really? I must have made quite an impression."

She slid into the seat and leaned back. How much should she reveal?

"Hmm." He grimaced. "By your hesitation, I was a jerk."

Yes, but... "I remember you and your brother singing in the talent show at camp."

"Yeah, we used to do that back in the day. There were a lot of talented kids there." He stared into his mostly-empty cup.

Good. He'd given her a reason to be vague with her explanation. "It's a long story but..." She stared across the room at her first guitar. "The bottom line is one of the performers that year broke my heart and I lost my sister for a while as a result."

"Ouch."

"It's not your fault." Or at least not totally. "I think the guy just got blinded by all the attention. Made me want to steer clear of that scene." Forever if she could, even if the music kept calling.

He swallowed hard. "I've definitely learned it the hard way lately, but the stage lights can blind you to truth and performing as a lifestyle tricks you into believing that you deserve that life. But when you get knocked off that pedestal, what do you have?"

Was that what had sent him to their door?

She cleared her throat. "Hopefully you still have your family. And your faith."

"Faith." He drained the last of his coffee, then twisted in his seat, pointing toward the far wall. "What's the story behind that guitar with the words on it?"

"Ah. That was my first guitar." She smiled at the memories of how God had redeemed her heartbreak even as her eyes took in the message about true light and faith. A truth she sometimes forgot when faced with her fears. "It's an Ed Stilley original."

***

"A who?" Tyler swiveled from the strange-looking instrument with the message that had changed his heart back to the pretty waitress sitting across from him.

"Ed Stilley. He died recently but he used to be a farmer and a preacher in a little place called Hogscald Holler down in Arkansas."

He snorted. "That sounds like a place in Arkansas."

"True." A genuine smile erased the earlier shadows from her eyes. "Dad grew up near there."

"So, this dude had a guitar—"

"Made a guitar." She tilted her head and her honey-colored hair brushed along her cheekbone. "Actually, he said he received a call from God to make instruments and it's estimated he made over 200 guitars, dulcimers, and fiddles from assorted scraps. Almost like he was a recycler on a mission to transform broken things and trash into music. And then he gave them all away, mostly to children. Like my dad."

"I thought you said it was *your* first guitar."

"It was both." Her smile faded. "He gave it to me in early high school when I was struggling. Taught me how to play."

There was more to that story than she was telling—like before when talking about the church camp—but at least he now knew they had music in common. On some level.

He hadn't been sure why he'd felt prompted to stop by the Way Stop today when he had his own coffee pot at the cabin, but being around people and now making a tentative friend in Grace had been a breath of fresh air after the heavy soul-searching of the past few days.

Tyler leaned back in his chair and twirled his now-empty coffee cup. "Do you still play?"

After a momentary pause, she raised her eyebrows. "Do you?"

He blinked. Of course he played. Well, not in Vegas where the show's band played the music and he just sang and performed the choreography. And not in the Rockin' the Decades show either.

"Actually..." He looked down at his hands. "I guess the last time I picked up an instrument was over three months ago." Had it truly been that long? And even then, it had been an electric guitar while performing with his family in Branson.

His fingers twitched with the suppressed urge to strum an acoustic again. To hear the pure tones resonate alongside his renewed faith with nothing standing in the way. "Do you think I could try out that Arkansas guitar to see how it sounds?"

Grace shifted on her chair, then stood. "Maybe a different time." She stared at the corner for a bit, then nodded as if she'd reached some sort of decision. "But if you visit my dad's workshop, he's got a similar version or two back there. In addition to giving lessons to the locals, he also makes more traditional style guitars during the winter months."

Her dad made guitars? In addition to the bait, boats, breakfast, and music lessons he'd seen advertised on a flyer beside the door? Did the mystery man run the kitchen, too?

Tyler bit his lip to stop his laughter. He couldn't wait to meet the multi-talented Mr. Mitchell. "How much do I owe you for the coffee?"

She waved a hand. "That cup's on the house."

"Thank you." He stood. "Do you mind pointing me in the direction of your dad's shop? I'd hate to stumble in the wrong door out here and meet somebody's shotgun."

That brought the smile back to her face just like he'd hoped.

"Once you head out the front door, turn left. Then left at the corner of the building past his studio." She pointed to the musical corner with the mystery side door, then swept her hand along the bait and boats wall toward the back corner. "Keep on going until you reach that corner and you'll see the path heading straight back into the woods and his workshop."

"Any shotguns to worry about?"

"None I'd tell you about." Grace winked—actually winked—before picking up his empty coffee cup and crossing the room to add it to a tub of dirty dishes. After hoisting the load, she backed into the swinging doors to the kitchen. "See you around sometime." And promptly disappeared.

With one last glance at the handmade guitar, Tyler pushed out the front door and made his way around the building. Like Grace had directed, a dirt path led between the trees to a rustic building about the size of his cabin.

The haphazard weatherbeaten exterior boards common to the Ozarks lowered his expectations, and yet through the open door he caught a glimpse of organized pegboards on a paneled wall above a workbench, the scent of sawdust and stain, and the melody of a familiar hymn played on a guitar.

Something—or Someone—drew him closer until he stood in the doorway with a full view of the gleaming instruments, the stereo speaker mounted in the corner, and the man sanding the distinctly-shaped body of a guitar while humming along to the music.

Hymns. Worship. His heritage.

And the peace on the man's face as he worked in such a place stirred something in Tyler's soul.

If only he could have the same confidence. To know where he fit in the intersection of music and faith. Oh, to be back on Granny's front porch strumming a guitar. To play again without the lights and smoke and microphones.

Only for the love of the music.

With nothing to hide behind.

Exposed.

And yet the vulnerability felt right, just like when on his knees with an open Bible. If only he could go back in time and make different choices that would honor his renewed faith in God.

"Are you just going to stand there or do you want to make yourself useful?"

Tyler blinked and found the man watching him with a hint of a smirk just like his daughter inside the Way Stop.

He stepped inside the door. "Mr. Mitchell? I asked about the Ed… guitar on the wall and Grace sent me back this way."

"Call me Luke." He pointed to a chair, a square of sandpaper, and a stick of wood. "Work in the direction of the grain and see if you can take off the rough edges."

The man might as well be speaking a foreign language, but Tyler sat as directed and made an attempt. After first watching the man carefully for a minute.

Soon the rhythmic swishing of the grit against the wood fell into time with the background music and Tyler's pulse slowed. He eyed the various pieces nearby on the workbench and could already see how they'd fit together.

His grandfather and great-grandfather had made their own instruments and for some crazy reason, Tyler wanted to do the same. It had to be from spending so much time in the woods the past few days, and yet he couldn't shake the feeling. "How complicated is it to make a guitar?"

"Any old guitar or one that resonates in tune with God's design?"

Tyler paused his sanding. "Does God design guitars?"

The older man chuckled. "I like to imagine that the Ultimate Creator had a plan when He put music in the hearts of His followers, but I think He lets us put our own stamp on the design." He tilted his head. "As long as we stay in the True Light of our Faith in God."

Tyler swallowed hard. "Are we still talking about guitars?"

"Yes and no. Because we're all just instruments in the hands of the Master Craftsman."

Once again they fell into silence as they worked. A few minutes later, Tyler rotated the piece and worked on the other side. Despite the slow progress, there was a noticeable difference in the shape of the wood.

And he could already feel the neck of the guitar in the palm of his hand. Smooth. Sturdy. And designed for a purpose.

Was God trying to teach him something?

"So, young Sherwood, what brings you here?"

Tyler's hands stilled. How did—?

Luke laughed. "I know who owns the cabin you're staying in and I went to school with your parents." He gestured for Tyler to resume sanding. "I might not know which of their brood you are or why you're hiding in the woods, but I do know God has a plan."

A plan. To bring him back home?

He cleared his throat. "I'm Tyler."

The man raised an eyebrow as if the name meant something. His thoughtful expression was followed a moment later with a nod. "Well, Tyler, if you're willing, I can help you craft an instrument that in the right hands can make beautiful music."

CHAPTER SEVEN

Tyler turned up the collar of his wool-lined coat against the mid-morning chill coming off the lake and hurried down the newly-worn path through the woods separating his cabin-away-from-home from Luke's workshop behind the Way Stop.

It was hard to believe he'd stayed in the area for so long, but after three weeks working with Luke in the shop, Tyler's guitar was almost done. In that time, he'd also spent hours helping the man work on other instruments and learning what went into creating a quality sound while simultaneously falling in love again with the simplicity of musical tone, harmonies, and lyrics.

Of course, they had also debated theology, politics, and even sports while working on the various guitars, but in addition to woodcrafting and musicianship, there were plenty of object lessons about faith all set to the background music of worship.

Gracie—as her father affectionately called her—was lucky to have been raised by such a man.

Just like God, the Master Craftsman, Luke had shown him the process and satisfaction of shaping something from nothing with his bare hands. Of removing the rough edges and unnecessary trimmings to get down to the core so the tone resonated. Of even—like the infamous Ed Stilley—reclaiming the junk or broken pieces the world discarded and fitting them into a design.

And while he'd been scavenging and shaping and sanding the pieces for his guitar, God had been whittling away at Tyler's misplaced priorities and shaping him into a new man.

An instrument in the hands of the Master.

But what would he do with what he'd learned once he returned to his normal life?

Time enough to think about the future later. Today, he planned to attach the neck to the body of the guitar. Then all that remained would be the hardware like the fret board and bridge, several coats of stain, a polish, and finally the strings.

Tyler shivered despite his coat and picked up the pace. However, as chilled as his fingers were, perhaps he should drop by the Way Stop first for coffee and another chat with Gracie.

Backwoods girls had never been his type before, but there was something genuinely appealing about her. Something real. He'd been reporting daily on his progress in the shop, but after catching her reading her Bible one morning during a slow period, their conversations had gotten progressively deeper until he counted her as probably his closest friend aside from his family.

And daily he counted his blessings that she'd shot down his flirting that first day, because otherwise he might never have taken another look.

Gracie Mitchell was a hidden gem and he couldn't get enough of her smile. There was something about her that drew his eyes...and his heart. He couldn't wait to get to know her better even if that meant revealing more of his broken self.

After rounding the corner of the building, Tyler ducked inside the Way Stop and scanned the room.

Gracie smiled at him, but since she was busy serving a few locals like the past few Saturdays, she pointed to the coffee pot to help himself.

He grinned. He'd been around too often if he'd been demoted from being waited on to self-service. But that was fine. He wouldn't change a thing.

Once he had a cup of the hot brew, he found an empty seat where he could see the guitars on the wall. And the recently empty spot since Luke had let him borrow an instrument until his was done.

Tyler rubbed his fingertips together. It had taken time to rebuild the callouses, but he'd already moved beyond strumming simple chords back to plucking individual strings to recreate melody lines.

Like the hymn playing in the background.

With a couple sips of coffee warming him from the inside out, he closed his eyes and imagined playing the various notes. Muscle memory was finally combining with his natural ear for notes in a God-inspired way.

"Hello, stranger." He opened his eyes to find Gracie had slipped into the chair across from him.

He shook his head. "How long do I have to live around here before I'm not an outsider?"

A smirk curved her lips. "Um, at least a couple years. But I can't imagine you living without proper heat for that long."

After needing to borrow tweezers and a needle to remove the splinters acquired feeding his fireplace more wood in the middle of the night, he'd confessed the truly rustic living conditions.

An unsettled feeling grew in his gut. There was a reason his great uncle closed up the cabin for the season and frozen water pipes were just the first symptom. Which meant he would not be able to spend the winter in Ridgedale.

That there would be a goodbye to Grace on the horizon. And a return to Branson.

Unless he started looking for an apartment or rental house in town so he could stay close but in comfort.

"Tyler?" She lowered her voice. "What are you really doing here?"

"Besides hiding from my family?" A quick glance around the room confirmed they were alone. Time to finally admit the truth. "I got lost."

She raised an eyebrow as if she wanted to fire off a smart remark but didn't. "Are you still trying to find your way?"

"Between the message on that guitar—" He pointed to the wall over her shoulder. "—a dusty Bible at the cabin, and your dad's daily object lessons, I'm on the right path home." The word triggered a deep longing.

"Where were you before coming here?"

"Vegas."

She snorted with laughter, then stopped. "You're serious."

"Ever hear of the television show *Making Music*?"

"A little." Her eyes widened. "You were on it?"

Obviously she wasn't watching the current episodes or else she'd have seen him.

He gave her the short version of the story from auditioning to packing up and moving only to discover his semi-girlfriend in the arms of their coach and the pre-determined results. "Everything fell apart. So, I did the only thing I could do. Came home. Except when I got here, I was too embarrassed to show my face." And the delay since then was only making that reunion more complicated.

"With a family like yours, how'd you get so lost in the first place?"

"I've been asking myself that same question for weeks, but I think it started back in high school." He winked to lighten the mood. "Don't laugh, but I had a very fragile ego."

Like he'd hoped, she burst into laughter anyway. "Your flirty eyebrow move is all an act?"

"Yep." There was a slight sting of truth. Apparently his ego hadn't gotten any tougher over the years, at least where a certain green-eyed girl was concerned.

"And the Elvis lip curl?" She attempted to duplicate the move and suddenly he could see how foolish he looked. Even if it had drawn attention to her kissable lips.

Heat flooded his face. "Yes. I'm an idiot."

"I refuse to comment on that assessment." She grinned. "But I have a hard time picturing you as an awkward, angsty teenager."

He shifted on the wooden chair. "Oh, you have no idea…"

***

"You can't leave me hanging like that." Grace leaned forward and rested her chin on one hand. "What happened back in high school?"

Tyler shook his head. "Only if you agree to tell me the rest of your camp story."

She froze. Could she take the risk and reveal her heartbreak? Maybe she could think of a different story to share instead? Except all other memories had fled.

All teasing faded from his eyes as they swept over her face, lingering for a fraction of a moment on her lips before rising to capture her gaze. "Please. I want to get to know the real Gracie Mitchell."

She felt vulnerable and exposed by the request, and yet she couldn't deny the emotional connection humming between them. She sighed. "It's a deal." She might regret it tomorrow, but when they shook on it, sparks shot up her arm and ignited her hopes that this time around things might work out.

He squeezed their joined hands, then released her and leaned back in his chair. "Once upon a time in high school, there was a boy with a fragile ego." He quirked his lips into a half smile. "He loved music and enjoyed performing with his large family at different church events around the state. But alas—"

"Alas?"

"Hush. This is my story." He smirked, but she could see he was using humor to mask the pain. And the vulnerability.

Knowing her turn was next, she refused to laugh no matter what fancy words he chose to use.

"Alas, the boy was lost in the middle of a large group. Not to mention he had an identical twin so people were always mixing them up. Like a typical teenager, he only wanted to be seen for himself."

She could relate to the twin thing herself. While life had sent her and Mercy in opposite directions for a season, she could relate to always being part of a duo and never an individual.

Tyler gazed off into the distance as if lost in thought.

Grace cleared her throat. "So, the boy who wanted to be seen…"

He blinked several times. "Ah, yes, one time during a concert, he spotted a girl in the audience who kept looking his way. A cute girl from his school. He made eye contact and smiled a few times just for her. After the show, she…"

"She found you and told you how amazing you were." His story was getting too close for comfort.

"True." He shrugged. "But she made a special point to compliment me on my solo." His lips twisted. "Except I hadn't sung a solo. My younger brother Nick had. I hadn't even been mistaken for my twin that time. But still, the attention was flattering and as she gushed on and on about how my voice gave her goosebumps and—" He clasped his hands under his chin and batted his eyelashes "—would live in her dreams forever, I went along with it. Ended up taking her out that night and enjoyed a few kisses."

She tapped a finger on her chin. "Exactly what part of that story is about a fragile ego?"

"I overheard her talking to a few friends later about how she'd kissed Nick Sherwood. After all that, she didn't even know it was me. Like we were interchangeable."

She winced at the raw pain in his voice.

"So, I vowed to stand out from the rest and be memorable." He looked down at his clasped hands now resting on the table top. "Performing suddenly became about being noticed and not about the music, emotion, or message. And the more people—girls—noticed the boy with the fragile ego, the more he craved the attention. And the more outrageous he behaved to keep eyes on himself, the further he got from the truth. And faith. Until poof, it all went up in smoke in Vegas…"

"And now?" She could see the genuine regret and recalled the blunt honesty in his tale.

He lifted his head and stared into her eyes. "But now he's seen the True Light. And after weeks spent reading the Bible and working in a wood shop, he feels like he's back to the music-loving faith-filled place he was in before all the distractions began."

"And he doesn't need the applause or the bright lights anymore?" Had he really changed? Was the real Tyler truly emerging? Because the new version in sweaters and jeans and genuine smiles had eased his way into her heart and given her foolish ideas of what might be.

"It's true. I don't need or even want to be noticed anymore." He waved a hand at the woods outside the window. "But hiding out here doesn't change the fact I have a lot to make up for."

"You do know that God's forgiveness covers your sins, right?"

"Yes. But the prodigal still had to walk the road home. And while his father welcomed and forgave him, the older brother didn't." A flash of worry in his eyes underscored his reluctance to finish the journey home.

God, pave the way for Tyler. May he find love and forgiveness waiting instead of—

"And now it's your turn."

"My turn?" She frowned.

"I told you my sob story and we made a deal."

Right. And they'd even shook on it.

They'd become good friends, but could she truly bare her heart to him? His story involved an unnamed girl, while hers...

Stalling for time, she stood. "It's kinda a long story and I do need to close up the Way Stop."

"I'll help, and then we can go for a walk while you talk." His expression left no room for argument.

Too soon, they were bundled up and strolling down the road toward the lake.

"As I recall, your story started with a girl at camp and performer breaking her heart."

She swallowed hard, then following his third person storytelling example from earlier, laid the foundation. "Once upon a time there was a freshman girl who had a crush on an upperclassman at her school. And she hoped that spending time at church camp over Spring Break would help him to notice her."

"Um, I hate to ask, but..." He frowned. "Was it me?"

So much for keeping that part of the story a secret. She sighed, then darted a glance at the man walking beside her. "Yes."

He swallowed hard as if preparing to face another of his mistakes, but then a hint of the old Tyler flashed in his eyes. "A crush, huh?"

Heat flooded her cheeks. "At least until I got crushed."

"Ouch." He sobered. "I wish I could remember what happened so I could truly apologize."

At least he was sorry. That had to count for something. But now that she'd started, she needed to finish. "Almost like your story, the girl watched the boy all through the concert and then approached him afterward. But not to gush about any solo. Rather she was impressed by his guitar playing and after mentioning her wish to learn how to play that well, he volunteered to show her a few tricks after the evening's ice cream social."

"Hmm. How noble of him."

Right. "While the other teens headed for the cafeteria and the promised dessert, I rushed back to my room. Combed my hair, brushed my teeth, applied lip gloss..."

He gave her a wolfish grin. "Because you never know when fresh breath matters."

She nodded, then stared into the distance as the painful part of the memory came next. "Then, prepared for anything and excited to spend a little time with her hero, she ran to the cafeteria and rounded the corner only to see the guy flirting with..." She swallowed hard.

"Uh-oh." Dread filled his voice as he obviously filled in the gaps of her story. "Someone else?"

"You could say that." Her sister. "And he didn't even have his guitar with him. When he saw me, he waved me over to join them, but it was obvious he was only interested in having a fan club. Not the music. Or me." So she'd left.

But not before Mercy had gone ballistic and caused a huge scene. As much as Grace's feelings were hurt, Mercy hadn't liked being mistaken for her twin either. And much like Tyler, had gone on to try to stand out in her own unique way starting with dying her hair.

"I'm so sorry." He hunched his shoulders and kicked at a rock.

"You're the one you asked for that story." She sighed at the misery on his face. "However, it all worked out because I found someone else to teach me how to play the guitar." And she'd gone on to become a quiet band nerd at school, disappearing into the background while Mercy made a name for herself and soaked up all the attention.

"There is that I suppose."

"True. Dad was a much better teacher."

"Really?" Tyler nudged her with his elbow. "I still know a few tricks."

She rolled her eyes. "He was less distracting for sure."

He stopped their progress with a hand on her arm, then turned to face her. "I can't imagine why I don't remember you from back then, but it's more-than-obvious I had to do some growing up. Maybe the timing wasn't right." His gaze warmed. "But now…"

"Now?" Why did she have to sound so breathless?

"Maybe God gave us both a second chance. Brought me here. Changed my life. And suddenly I could see myself falling for you." He closed the distance between them and the brush of his lips on hers soon turned into a real kiss.

A rush of tingles spread throughout her body to the point she was almost dizzy with sensation. With emotion. With…

But wait.

Could see himself falling wasn't the same as a true declaration.

Grace wrangled her foolish thoughts back into submission and stepped back.

It might be wise to protect her heart.

CHAPTER EIGHT

Late Tuesday morning, Tyler let himself into Luke's workshop and turned on the space heater. Rubbing his chilled hands together, he crossed to the main workbench. All his guitar needed was a final coat of wax, a polish, and another tuning.

He pulled over a stool and picked up a piece of cheesecloth. It was hard to believe that just a few weeks ago this instrument had been a pile of scraps in the corner. He shook his head. He'd been the same discarded mess after the Vegas disaster.

After folding the cloth, he dipped into the can of wax and rubbed a thin layer over the seam between the two types of wood he'd chosen. He especially liked the contrast in the grains which made the instrument uniquely his instead of looking like one that came out of a cookie-cutter-style manufacturing facility.

As he buffed the excess wax from the back of the guitar, his fingers caught the dent in the wood near the curved waist. The nick was the result of a mishap when attaching the binding, and while he'd tried to sand it out, he now appreciated the subtle reminder that everyone had a few imperfections. After all, it was the scars that held the best stories.

He rolled his eyes. If Gavin could see him now waxing poetic…while waxing.

Tyler turned the instrument to work on another area, very aware of the extra weight of the industrial spring wedged inside. It seemed the original Ed Stilley legacy of using bits of trash for extra resonance continued, but as Luke said, it was the heart that made one unique and only the craftsman knew what lay within.

God, You have searched me and know my inward parts.

He smiled. Scripture and truth all at once. But hopefully—prayerfully—his heart would resonate with the true light of faith even deeper than the spring amplified the sounds created with his guitar.

Lost in thought, Tyler continued applying wax, rubbing off the excess, and then buffing the surface to a high sheen. However, when he reached the neck, he paused to run a finger over the transformative words about true faith and light that he had etched along the top edge. Right where he could see them while playing the guitar.

Never again would he lose sight of what truly mattered in life.

"Am I ever glad you already turned on the heat."

Tyler turned to see Gracie's dad warming his hands near the heater. "I knew you had a couple lessons this morning, but couldn't wait to get started."

Luke waved a hand in dismissal. "I told you to make yourself at home here. But while the heat is nice, I sure could use a little music that doesn't sound like squawking seagulls." He crossed to the stereo, dug around in the pile there, and finally inserted a disc.

Seagulls? Tyler shook his head. Then again, he'd heard the beginning students and out-of-tune strings plucked randomly really did grate on one's eardrums.

Luke approached and put a hand on his shoulder. "Seems to me you're about done here."

Did he mean that in more than one way? Because of the gleaming instrument in his hands or because Thanksgiving was in two days and Tyler really should be...

Luke moved on to check the dried glue on a different creation, then removed the clamps. Tyler dipped into the wax again while in the background an acoustic guitar played along with... Was that a computer synthesized drum beat?

He stopped polishing and listened closer, picking out the various instruments. Some were live and others obviously manufactured sounds, but somehow they blended into a distinctive sound. He raised his eyebrows. Whoever had done the musical arrangement was a genius.

A woman began to sing and her one-of-a-kind voice raised goosebumps across his skin. The purity of the sound and resonant tones drew him in. Followed by the realization that the lyrics spoke of a life of worship. Of awe at the Creator. Of the romance of the ages.

He blinked back tears he hadn't known were forming. Now *this* was music as God intended.

"Like it, do you?" He glanced over to see Luke watching him with a wistful smile. "She reminds me a lot of my late wife. Roxie sang all the time no matter what she was doing."

Roxie. A week or so ago, Luke had mentioned losing his wife to cancer when Gracie was young. Normally he'd let Luke direct the flow of conversation, but first, he had to know. "Who's the artist?"

Luke's smile changed to one of pride. "She's one of my students who's going to make it big someday soon. I have a feeling that with her original music, she's going to be a star."

Just watch, I'm going to make you a star.

The words he'd overheard in Vegas soured his stomach. "Being a star isn't always a good thing."

"Why do you say that?"

"I wanted to be a star once." Still did if he were being brutally honest. "But in the pursuit, I forgot who I was supposed to be and it cost me more than I knew was possible."

His family. His self respect. And even confidence in his ability to sing or play.

Luke shot him a stern look as if gazing into his soul. "I believe it's possible to make it big without losing yourself. But it all starts at the core of who you are. Why do you sing? To be noticed? To build up your worth? If you're not enough without the music, you'll always be chasing the wrong things."

Just like the Audience of One his brother Nick used to talk about.

"Could you ever be happy in the background?" One last quirk of the eyebrows to drive home his point, and then Luke turned back to his work, humming along to the music.

Could he?

On the stereo, the music switched to a new-but-similar song with even more lyrics that wove into Tyler's heart and made him take an honest look at himself.

Like he'd told Gracie on Saturday, he had definitely played for the attention. As a means to the end of fame and to boost his self-esteem as an individual. However, he'd heard others— like his parents—talk about playing for the love of the music and the way it touched their souls.

And maybe back in the very beginning he'd enjoyed the music for its own sake.

But now, who was he without the music? A bearded recluse. Who spent his days in a workshop making instruments and filled his lonely evenings in a freezing-cabin playing hymns on a borrowed guitar.

Perhaps music was part of how God had designed him?

But, he'd never composed an original song in his life. His talent came in performing what someone else had written. Did that mean he could be happy in the background?

Maybe it was time to let someone else take the lead.

Someone else.

"Where You lead, I will follow." The mystery singer's voice echoed the cry of his heart.

Yes, God. I'll follow. Lead me where You want me to go.

Then as the melody of the chorus repeated, Tyler found himself humming along and wishing he was alone so he could attempt to recreate the notes.

Luke chuckled. As if he knew a secret.

Suddenly both awkward and embarrassed around Gracie's father, Tyler made a show of wiping the last surface and putting the lid back on the can of wax. "Other than a final tuning that could remind you of the seagulls you're avoiding, my guitar is done."

He eyed the guitar with a deep sense of satisfaction. The excitement at completing the project was an addicting feeling.

Luke nodded. "It is."

Right. Both exciting. And done.

But the unanswered question hung in the air. Without the guitar, what reason did Tyler have to keep coming back?

He shook off the thought and instead eyed the instrument in his hands. This needed a celebration of some sort.

But what? He could head to his cabin to play his own guitar and solidify that melody line in his memory…or since he was already here, detour to the restaurant for a cup of coffee and a sandwich as his excuse to see the woman he couldn't get off his mind.

Especially after their kiss on the road.

Who was he without music? He grinned. He was also a man falling in love with a beautiful woman with a heart of gold.

"I'm going to go show it to Gracie."

"You do that." Luke turned back to his work, hiding whatever he really thought about Tyler and his daughter. At least the man didn't ask what Tyler's intentions were.

Then again, he probably already knew.

Heat bloomed in his face. After grabbing his coat, Tyler picked up the evidence of his hard work and hurried from the room, leaving the other man alone with the compelling music.

Tyler took the path along the side of the Way Stop building with the previous melody still playing in his head along with the lyrics of following wherever God led.

Well, God had led him here four weeks ago.

To Gracie. And the grace of being forgiven and returning to his heritage of faith. But also to Gracie.

His smile grew. He couldn't wait to see where God led with her too.

But no matter what, music would somehow always be a part of his future. At least it would be after he came out of hiding and reconnected with his family... Eventually.

Assuming he cleared that uncomfortable hurdle, where would Gracie fit into his life in Branson?

Actually, she'd said her dad taught her to play the guitar. And he'd love nothing more than to play together with her someday. Or would she be embarrassed? It didn't matter how much of a beginner she was, because he just wanted to share that part of himself with her.

Because the more he prayed, returned to his faith roots, and fell in love with music again the way his family used to play on Granny's porch, the more he was hoping for a future with Grace.

CHAPTER NINE

E very time the bell clanged all morning, Grace had looked over expecting Tyler. Only to be disappointed.

It was a good thing Mercy wasn't around yet to see her acting like a blushing fool. But her sister and nephew would be here tomorrow afternoon and then the teasing would begin.

She was in the middle of ringing up a lunch order plus a few snacks from the grocery area when Tyler finally entered. Butterflies swirled in her stomach, but she fought to make small talk with the customer like normal. "Getting ready for a road trip?"

Except while bagging the man's purchases, she was very aware that Tyler was headed toward her instead of his usual table. And he was carrying a guitar.

"Sure am. Hope the storm holds off. Traveling for Thanksgiving can get tricky with all the travelers on the road." The man pulled out his wallet and passed over two twenties before picking up the plastic bag. "Keep the change as your tip."

She blinked. "Thank you."

By the time she'd opened the cash drawer and slipped the appropriate change into the pocket of her jeans, the lone customer was long gone and Tyler stood in his place.

Holding out the guitar like a turkey on a platter.

"Tada. It's done."

"Congratulations!" She eyed the instrument, tallying the distinguishing characteristics she'd seen during her too-frequent trips to the workshop. Trips that had earned her teasing from Dad at home and more than a few honest conversations about relationships and falling in love.

Conversations where Dad had given his nod of approval and agreed that the new Tyler was real and worth having in her life.

"What do you think?" Tyler lowered the guitar to the counter.

Her fingers itched to stroke the wood. To strum the strings. "It's gorgeous. But does it sound as good as it looks?"

"Better."

Grace glanced up to see his wide smile and twinkling eyes. As tempting as the instrument was, she'd much rather stroke his beard. To feel the soft hairs that had tickled her face during their kiss three days ago.

The kiss that had caused several sleepless nights, a distracted church service, and countless wishes for a repeat.

And blushes like the one currently heating her face. Again.

He winked and then his gaze dipped to her lips. "I'm in the mood to celebrate. And there's nothing sweeter than you."

Before she could catch her breath, he'd crossed the distance and captured her mouth with a searing kiss. A well-practiced kiss but one full of emotion.

Emotion for her.

She lifted a hand to cradle his cheek as she leaned into their connection and one kiss turned into three.

No about to fall in love for her. She was head over heels and beyond with Tyler Sherwood of all people. But not the old Tyler from her youth. This new and improved version was a better man than she'd ever dreamed he could become.

And wonder of wonders, he seemed to really like her, too.

The bell on the door clanged once again and Tyler ended their public display of affection as the deep bantering voices of two regular diners filled the room. Good thing they knew to seat themselves because she needed a moment to catch her breath.

"Gracie?" Tyler's voice came out in a husky whisper. "I love you."

She gasped. "Truly? I—"

He cut her off with a quick kiss, then cleared his throat. "We'll pick this up later. In the meantime, I'll let you take care of your customers. And I'd like a club sandwich and a cup of coffee whenever you get a chance." With that, he picked up his guitar and retreated to his usual table.

As if she was supposed to function as a decent employee while hyper-aware of her tingling lips, their audience, and the unspoken promise in his declaration.

The bell rang yet again and a family entered. Since she didn't recognize any of them, they'd probably rented a nearby cabin for Thanksgiving. And wouldn't be as understanding with a delay as the regulars.

But as she scurried around taking and filling orders, pouring drinks, and brewing another batch of coffee, it was increasingly difficult to ignore the fact Tyler was tuning her preferred instrument like a professional.

And the equally disturbing fact that she found the sight of him with the instrument in his hands almost as breathtaking as his earlier kisses.

For the first time in several years, inspiration flooded her mind with new melodies begging to be played. New lyrics demanding to be written and set to music. But this time, it was not a love song to her Heavenly Father surging through her veins.

If he asked, she'd promise him a lifetime. Of laughter. Of love. Of music.

If only she didn't have responsibilities to serve the Way Stop customers and could instead devote her days to music and music alone. Perhaps Dad was right and she should at least knock on a few doors before settling for a teaching career.

What would Tyler think if he knew she had other options?

Her attention drifted to the stereo in the corner where a month ago Dad had played her disc and revealed that he'd sent her demo tracks to a friend to share with his contacts in Nashville. What would the professionals have to say about her music?

She rubbed a hand over her churning stomach and ducked into the kitchen. While recent events made her wish she could perform her music, she still didn't know how to hold onto her identity if she ever set foot on a stage.

Not only that, Tyler didn't know she'd done more than learn how to play the guitar. That she, too, had been hiding here in the woods.

He needed to know. And soon. Especially if he was the one to inspire the album's worth of music currently on repeat in her mind. And hopefully the fact she'd waited this long to ask for professional career advice would set her apart from the likely hoards of other wannabe singers who'd approached him in the past.

God, a little wisdom here?

Perhaps she could break the ice of that momentous conversation by actually asking to play his guitar. A peace settled around her heart. Yes. She'd open the door to the topic of her personal music with a song and trust God to guide the rest of their conversation.

Except over the next hour she never got the chance. There were still too many customers around by the time Tyler was finished with his meal.

He shrugged, left cash on the table for his food even though both she and her dad had told him several times he didn't need to, then with one last heated glance her direction, disappeared out the front door with his new guitar.

With her sister's move home and all the extra meal preparations tomorrow, she probably wouldn't see him until after Thanksgiving. Especially since like the additional visitors today, he too would be traveling home for the holiday.

Could he hold onto his new identity? Or would he change again once he was back home?

Maybe she should hold onto her heart and dreams awhile longer until she'd seen the proof. But until she knew for sure, there was nothing to stop her from working on the new songs Tyler had inspired.

CHAPTER TEN

Tyler dumped the contents from yet another can of soup into the battered pan and turned on the gas burner. The dubious label pictured large chunks of chicken and vegetables but reality was much…smaller. Still, it was the closest he'd get to anything turkey related today.

Even a frozen dinner would have been worth the splurge if his uncle had a microwave at the cabin, but Tyler wasn't willing to risk the indoor air quality by attempting to heat a paper carton inside the oven and starting a fire.

He'd learned that lesson several weeks ago and it was far too cold outside to sleep with the windows open again.

A few minutes later, he poured the hot soup into a bowl and smirked. In honor of Thanksgiving, he was getting fancy instead of eating it out of the pan. Mom would be proud.

Oh, how he missed her cooking. Her hugs. Her love.

He carried his meal to a seat in front of the roaring fire and let the warmth seep into his bones as he studied the cabin that had become a home of sorts. His time within the rustic walls was about over. And not just because of the recent annoyance of feeding the fire twenty-four hours a day to keep the pipes from freezing inside the drafty cabin.

Yesterday, even with the spotty cell service, he'd finally searched the network's website for an update about *Making*

Music. The recorded episodes had been airing on schedule, but by this time next week, the whole world would know the truth that his group—he—had been eliminated from the competition.

And despite the fact he'd been hiding from them for weeks, he still wanted—needed—his family to hear the news directly from him instead of second hand.

Perhaps he shouldn't have ignored the group text invitation he'd received and joined his family for the holiday. Except instead of being lost in the crowd, he had a feeling he would have been in the spotlight of attention. And questions.

No. He simply couldn't ruin the gathering for everyone else. Despite the past, he'd much rather be noticed for himself and not his onstage drama.

He scooped a bite of rapidly cooling soup. Canned chicken just didn't taste the same. Didn't even smell the same.

His stomach revolted and he set the half-eaten bowl aside while trying to ignore the possibility there might be a real turkey cooking at the Mitchell's house right now.

Not that the Way Stop was open. He'd seen the paper sign in the window announcing their closure for several days and despite their kisses and his feelings for Grace—and all the time spent with Luke at the workshop—he hadn't felt comfortable dropping the hint that he'd be alone for Thanksgiving.

Which also made it impossible to simply knock on their front door and invite himself over for a meal.

Especially since he'd also seen a strange car with Arkansas plates parked at their house since yesterday. Interrupting their time with guests just wasn't his style anymore. Because if he wouldn't crash his own family's gathering, no way would he show up uninvited anywhere else.

After seeking to be alone for so many weeks, why was he now craving company?

God? What's going on? What are You doing with my life?

A feeling grew deep inside that something was about to change. And finally for the better.

Where am I supposed to be? Here with Gracie and her dad and simple music? Back in Branson on the stage?

Thoughts of music reminded him of the mystery artist's voice singing the lyrics he still couldn't get out of his head. *Where You lead, I will follow.*

Ignoring his abandoned meal, he crossed the small room to retrieve his guitar. Perhaps he could recreate the melody from memory. In addition to keeping his fingers warm, the musical exercise would pass the time and take his mind off the uncomfortable fact he was still alone and far from home.

And the focus on the powerful lyrics was a good as a prayer.

At least for today, his path was clear.

CHAPTER ELEVEN

Grace sang along to the classic Christmas tunes on the radio as she unboxed more decorations for The Way Stop.

The bell on the door clanged and she spun around. "Sorry, we're—"

"Closed. I know." Tyler shut the door and turned with a smile. "But when I saw the lights on, I couldn't help stopping by."

A giddy feeling fluttered in her chest. They were alone and wouldn't be interrupted. After all, Mercy had driven to Springfield of all places for Black Friday shopping while Dad and little Jake were working on a puzzle.

Tyler glanced around the room but she couldn't take her eyes off the dark chocolate color of his sweater that matched his eyes. The width of his shoulders and the fit of his jeans. Lord, have mercy, the man was too handsome for his own good.

"Christmas, already?" He swiveled to face her with a quirked eyebrow.

Her face heated at being caught staring and she quickly focused on the garland in her hands. "Never hurts to decorate when I won't be interrupted by testy customers wanting fresh coffee."

"I have a feeling you still have coffee brewed even without customers to drink it." There was teasing in his voice.

He knew her too well. She looked up to find him three steps closer. "I do." Now there was a loaded phrase if ever she heard one. She cleared her throat. "But you'll have to earn it."

"Hmm. I sense a challenge."

"Ever decorated before or did you leave that to your mom and sisters?"

He chuckled. "Truth. We guys got to haul in the tree and make sure it was straight. Then head right back outdoors to hang the lights."

She waved her handful of garland at the hooks already positioned above the windows. "Just one more swag over this window, then I could use some tree expertise." She nodded toward the large box beside the bait counter. "We usually set it up there since it's out of the way."

"And bait is out of season." He shook his head. "But artificial, Gracie? Really?"

"Did you see any real ones for sale yet? Especially any living ones that might survive all the way until Christmas even if I didn't have a history of killing plants?"

"No. And no. I see your point." He reached for the garland and their fingers brushed, sending sparks up her arm.

And reminding her of last night's giggle-and-whisper fest with her twin all triggered by an innocent question about whether or not Grace had her eye on any cute boys in the area.

Tyler climbed on top of a chair to hang the garland, putting the seat of his jeans closer to her eye level. Heat climbed her face again and she spun away.

Why had she ever thought being alone would be a good idea?

She pushed the empty garland box across the floor to join the other boxes waiting for a return trip to the storage room. By the time she'd opened the first box of tree decorations, she had her emotions back under control and was focused on the next task.

As if sensing her mood, Tyler ditched his coat, pushed up his sleeves, positioned the tree stand, and then helped her wrestle the unwieldy branches into a natural-looking arrangement. Once the strands of lights were untangled, checked, and woven into place, Grace sensed the home stretch and reached for the last box of ornaments.

While Tyler searched for the coffee.

At least he returned from the kitchen with two steaming mugs.

"Aren't you going to help me finish?"

He pulled out a chair and gave an exaggerated sigh of relief. "Haven't I earned this cup yet? After all, my previous decorating resume only included setting up trees and hanging lights."

She rolled her eyes. "Are you saying that garland earlier was above and beyond the call of duty?"

"If you say so." He smirked, then took a sip of his coffee. "However, maybe I can convince you to take a break?"

The rich aroma of coffee wafted across the room and called to her like a siren. "Okay. You win. But fair warning, I might try to talk you into adding ornament hanging to that resume in exchange."

"Duly noted." Tyler nudged the second mug her direction.

She plopped into a seat and sighed. She'd been going nonstop since dawn when she awoke with the lyrics to yet another song in her mind. Sitting awhile would be a relief. Not to mention the caffeine would help restore her energy.

"Amazing how fake greenery can make even a bait shop look festive."

She rolled her eyes. "How long are you going to hold our artificial tree against me? Forever?"

His eyes darkened and swept over her face. "Forever is a very long time. I think I'll reserve that for the really important things."

I promise you a lifetime and forever. I promise you...

Tyler snapped his fingers in front of her eyes. "Hey, where'd you go? For a moment you really zoned out."

She blinked. "Guess I really need the caffeine." And a better way to break the news he had inspired a love song. If only she had the courage to face that music.

But that wasn't now. She took a long sip and scrambled for a safe topic change. "How was Thanksgiving with your family?"

"I don't know."

How was that possible? Oh. "You mean it's a complicated mix of good and bad?" They'd had a few adjustments of their own yesterday as Dad tried to parent Jake and Mercy put her foot down.

He looked down at his cup and squirmed a little. "Complicated, yes. But I didn't go."

She stared. "Why ever not? What's wrong? Don't you miss them?"

He sighed. "Yes, I miss them. And before you ask, yes, I was invited." He shifted his cup between his hands. "But they still think I'm in Vegas…"

Her mind scrambled to fill in the gaps. Right. He'd been embarrassed to admit his failure and came here instead. "And you're still hiding?"

He raised his eyes. "Not for much longer. But humble pie is hard enough to swallow without doing it in front of the entire clan."

She knew enough about the vast Sherwood family tree to sympathize. "Well, if I'd known you were going to be around here, you could have eaten with us. Met my sister and her little boy."

"I would have liked that."

Meeting Mercy? Or spending time with her? Grace fought for a casual tone as she tested the waters. "Oh, I'm sure you'll run into her eventually since she'll be around this area for a while."

His lips curved into a familiar half-smile. "I would have liked spending more time with *you*." His gaze dropped to her lips for an instant before he leaned back, as if resisting the temptation. "But if you really want me to meet your sister…?"

Her pulse settled back into place and she shrugged. "Too bad she's doing the Black Friday shopping thing today."

He shuddered. "I hate shopping."

"Me, too. And crowds only make it worse." But she remembered another part of last night's talk with Mercy. "However, I do need to run up to Branson later. Thought I'd get some highlights." She'd grown used to the shorter style and was ready to spruce it up, especially for the holidays. And for Tyler.

He tilted his head and stared at her hair. "Nothing too drastic, I hope. I kinda like my blonde beauty just the way she is."

His compliment sent heat to her face and delicious tingles straight to her heart.

"However, if you're set on turning even more heads than mine, I've got a cousin who works in a salon. I could give you her number."

"Sure." While she wouldn't reveal where she'd gotten the number, it wouldn't hurt to get to know more of his family, would it? Or would she be intimidated by them? Grace swallowed her nerves. "What's your family like?" Just in case kissing Tyler in the woods led to something more official.

"Big. Loud. All up in each other's business."

She laughed. "Yeah. I got a dose of that myself yesterday, but I kept reminding myself it's only because they love me."

"True. But as much as I used to want the attention on stage, the hot seat with the family is something I'd rather do without." He got a far-away look in his eyes. "I used to hate getting lost in the crowd of cousins, but now I think I'd like being just one of the bunch. That's something my parents were good at."

"They don't stand out as the famous ones?" She seemed to recall David and Patricia Sherwood had been singing together long before their children joined them onstage.

He snorted. "Not hardly. It's actually a source of good-natured ribbing between Dad's siblings. In fact, I believe the family connections and accountability kept them grounded."

He looked thoughtful for a moment. "And they do the same for the others who've become successes in other fields. My Granny always made a point of pushing all of us to use our gifts for God's glory wherever that took us."

Something Dad had hammered home over pumpkin pie after Mercy had asked if they'd heard anything back about her demo tape. But now, Tyler had opened the door for her to ask for a little advice.

She cleared her throat. "How did your parents balance using their musical gifts on a stage but stay connected to family and their faith? Because I think that's something you—"

"Should have learned?" He raised an eyebrow.

She winced. "Maybe. But I really want—"

"Relax. You're not asking anything I haven't wrestled with myself over the past several weeks."

"Feel like sharing your conclusions?" Maybe she'd get further as a sounding board than as if asking for herself.

"When they started out, they were the stereotypical starving artists who needed family support in order to survive. Especially when they spent months on the road singing in hole-in-the-wall venues and staying in dive hotels because that's all they could afford. As their careers grew, they never lost sight of where they'd come from."

"Makes sense."

"I guess I was born with a silver spoon because I don't really remember those early days as being hard on our family. Especially since whenever they'd leave on tour or to record a new album, we kids got to stay with our grandparents."

"And get spoiled?"

"More like get smothered with chores and cousins." He chuckled. "But about the time my little sister Robin was born, they gave up the tours in favor of a steady gig in one theater. Probably gave up a lot of money, too, but that's also when we kids started singing with them."

"But they gained more family time together."

"In rehearsals and on stage and at home. Yes. Lots of family together time." He rolled his eyes. "I'm sure we drove my mother crazy more often than not, but with a home base here, we were still around our extended family."

"And along the way they ended up running their own theater instead of recording more albums."

"The music business has changed over the years. Used to be that radio stations helped to sell albums, but with all the streaming services now, musicians rely on tours and concerts for the majority of their income. And that's why shows are getting flashier with lights and fog and intricate choreography to attract bigger crowds. Unless you're a Christian artist with a focus on the message of the music, it seems like you can't tour with just a guitar anymore." Tyler shifted in his chair as if the topic was getting too close for comfort.

For both of them.

He pushed aside his empty coffee cup and stood. "Well, I think I've stalled about all I can, but it can't be that hard to hang ornaments on a tree."

Grace shook her head at the subject change, but followed him to the open box. "You just have to—"

"Are these fishing hooks?" Tyler held the metal hanger at the top of a red-glittered ball. "Isn't this taking the bait shop theme a bit too far?"

A giggle escaped her lips. "Well, I've seen many a beginner fisherman get his line caught on a tree branch when trying to cast."

He placed a hand over his heart as if wounded. "Were you there when my uncles tried to teach me?"

"Quit stalling." She pointed at the open box. "Now, get hanging. Just try to scatter a variety around the tree with smaller ornaments toward the top and the bigger ones near the bottom."

"Yes, ma'am." With a wink her direction, he actually dove into the task with gusto. Leaving her with time to process what he'd said about recording contracts and tours.

It actually sounded like more of a grind than a glamorous vacation. If anything came of her demo tape, maybe she could perform after all without getting too full of herself and thinking she deserved the star treatment. Or maybe she'd need to bring her dad along.

Or Tyler? No. That was silly. He'd never leave his family behind or his own chance to shine.

Or would he?

"Hey, Gracie? You got any mistletoe in any of these boxes?"

CHAPTER TWELVE

Grace tossed her purse into the passenger seat and slid behind the wheel of her car. Turned out Tyler's cousin had taken the weekend off, but the substitute stylist had done a great job.

She couldn't help peeking at herself in the rear-view mirror. Not too dark, but a few reddish strands now wove between her natural mixture of blonde and light brown. And the color seemed to make her green eyes sparkle even more.

Or maybe that was love.

A lot had changed in the past five weeks. Her appearance for one. But that was only the surface.

She had reunited with Tyler, become friends, and was now willing to take a risk on her future. Willing to consider possibilities instead of waiting for a teacher to retire. To let Mercy build a home in Ridgedale for her son while Grace flew as far as Branson or beyond.

The dream pounded on her door. Especially since she'd been writing music again. And as if the dam had broken, she'd written more in the past week than in the last two years combined.

And wonder of wonders, she knew the new songs were some of her best. With Mercy working at the Way Stop today,

Grace might find a little time to record a few rough tracks and capture more of the ideas while they were fresh.

She started the engine but before she could put the car in reverse, her phone rang. She fished the device out of her purse.

An unknown number. From Nashville.

Breath caught in her lungs as her heart pounded. Rejections were usually delivered via anonymous email, right? But good news would forever change her life.

Please, God? Give me courage.

With a shaky hand, she swiped to answer. "Hello?"

"Gracie Mitchell?"

"This is she." Only family—and recently Tyler—called her Gracie but it had a nice ring to it. If she needed a stage name…

"This is Richard Brent with Brent-Hill Records. I got your demo tape. Did you really do all the performing and arranging?"

She could be offended, but even her professors had questioned her assignment. "I did. It started out as a project for my audio techniques class but then I expanded it on my own."

"I have to say I'm quite impressed. You've got something special."

"Thank you." The words came out in a rush and then air refused to fill her lungs. How many people died from hyperventilating while getting good news?

"If you're available, I would like to set up a meeting early next week to discuss your options." The man rambled on as she somehow managed to grunt or uh-huh at the appropriate times. Instead of buying the rights to a few songs or hiring her to mix tracks at the studio, he was truly talking about a recording contract. A multi-album recording contract. And an introductory tour with a few very well-known artists.

Grace pinched her arm—hard—then winced. Nope. Not a dream.

Just a life-changing, up-ending, never-be-the-same phone call launching her into the future faster than a race car at the starting line of the Daytona 500.

"You, uh, said something about, uh, a meeting?" Her voice squeaked. So much for sounding like a professional.

He chuckled. "I'm sure you have—or will have—lots of questions before signing anything. But I'll do whatever I can to ease your concerns, including flying out there for a few days to meet with you and your family. Would Tuesday morning for you? Say around ten o'clock?"

The music industry big shot was clearing his calendar to come to her turf? Tears blurred her vision. He must really like her music.

She cleared the emotion from her throat. "I'll talk to my dad, but that should work." No doubt Dad would close the Way Stop before letting anything interfere with that appointment.

"Definitely take some time to think and pray about it, then give me a call on this, my personal number, to let me know your availability and where you'd prefer to meet. You can call any time. And Gracie, please know that while I'm on a mission to sign you, you're only agreeing to see the offer in writing and clarify the details. There's no obligation on your part to take this any further."

"I appreciate that." Especially since she hadn't had a coherent thought since her phone rang. "I'll be in touch."

After ending the call, Grace took several deep breaths. Until the faint buzzing in her head and hands stopped.

At long last, she pulled out of the lot and turned for home.

Who knew that dreams coming true could be so petrifying and energizing at the same time? Or release a swarm of butterflies.

Dad would say he'd told her so. But what would Tyler say? The butterflies fluttered for a different reason.

It was time to face the music. And well past time to approach the professional and admit her side-hustle dream.

***

Tyler had waited long enough.

He needed to see Gracie, even though they already had plans for their first official dinner date later that evening.

Despite the cold weather, he cut through the woods instead of driving. After bursting through the door, he took in the decorations—including the thoroughly-tested mistletoe—and the few diners in the restaurant section before spotting Gracie who was rearranging canned goods on the shelves.

Even from his position near the door, he could see her mostly-red hair with the multiple streaks that almost matched the purplish tones in her untucked flannel shirt.

The color might take some getting used to, but no matter what he was going to support her decision. "I thought you were just going to get a few highlights, not a dye job." Proud of the casual tone in his voice, he started her direction.

Unless she hated it. And then he'd offer a shoulder to cry on.

She turned with a slight frown. Her eyes swept over his face and beard before she finally smiled. Except it wasn't the same sweet expression he'd become used to, but more flirty. With a hard edge in her eyes.

What had happened to her? "Gracie?"

Her eyes widened and her face paled. "Not again."

"What?" Now he was the one who was truly confused.

"You thought I was Grace. Just like back in high school."

This wasn't Gracie? He took a closer look and felt like a fool.

She stepped forward. "I'm Mercy. Her—"

"Sister." And twin. Identical twin. As one of a pair himself, he should have known better. But when had he met twins back in high school?

Oh.

He stumbled to the closest chair and put his head in his hands. When Gracie had told him about her crush on him at camp and asking for guitar playing tips, he hadn't remembered the incident. But it turned out she'd spared him the most humiliating detail.

The other girl he'd flirted with was her own sister. Her identical twin. As if they were interchangeable. Something he was all too familiar with.

And while Gracie had quietly retreated to let her dad teach her guitar, Mercy had caused quite the scene at camp and beyond. And the nickname he'd bestowed to deflect from his accidental blunder had earned her a reputation she hadn't bothered to live down.

Something clinked near his elbow and he glanced up to find a cup of coffee…and Mercy. "Don't worry. I'm not going to make a scene and I'm not going to get in the way of your relationship with Gracie."

"She reminded me about that day at camp, but left out a big part of the story." He waved a hand between them. "And since then, she never mentioned a twin. Just a sister."

The substitute waitress gave a short laugh. "She's always tried not to hurt people's feelings. I bet she purposely never mentioned my name either."

"That would have helped." Although the wild reputation of Lord-have-Merrrcy Mitchell wasn't one Gracie would voluntarily link herself to. "However, now that I have the chance, I have to say that I'm so sorry for my part in—"

She waved off his apology, then after a quick glance around the room, took a seat across from him. "I made my own choices. People think that twins like being mistaken for each other, but—"

"We want to be known for ourselves." He pulled the coffee closer just to have something to do with his hands.

"Exactly. If it hadn't been that incident at camp, it would have been something else to send me on my prodigal journey."

A smile tugged at his lips. "Seems you and I have a lot in common."

"You're a single parent surviving a divorce and rebuilding your life, too?"

He winced. "Maybe I didn't go that far."

"But you did end up ditched in Vegas." She raised an eyebrow and smirked. "Gracie told me, but Dad said you've changed a lot since you ended up here."

"That's true. Except my family doesn't know about the Vegas part yet. Or any of the rest of it."

A second quirked eyebrow joined the first. "Oh, do tell."

He laughed. "I think you've probably weaseled most of it out of your family gossip source, but the truth is I began my slide back in high school while trying to stand out from the crowd. I wanted to be famous for myself. But the pursuit finally backfired and I've been hiding out here while trying to figure out how to admit my mistakes and beg for forgiveness."

"If your family is anything like their reputation in town, there won't be much begging involved."

"True. But that opening confession is still stuck in my throat and every night I go to bed thinking I'll make that first phone call tomorrow."

"I'd call you an idiot, except I know the feeling too well." Mercy rolled her eyes. "After my Goth phase in high school, I ended up as the stereotypical party girl in college. The knocked-up party girl whose values growing up wouldn't let her just eliminate the problem. Long story short, I ended up in a disaster of a marriage to a man who never wanted to be a father. Jake was not quite a year old when the divorce was final."

"I'm sorry." At least there weren't any permanently visible consequences to his own acts of rebellion.

"Don't be." Mercy waved off his words. "I've since gotten back on track, graduated from cosmetology school, and moved back home so I can be close to family. But I'm thankful for the hard times because it wasn't until I hit rock bottom that I began to crave God's attention instead of man's and began to truly understand God's mercy and accept His grace."

Mercy and Grace. Two sisters with names to remind him of God's character.

He chuckled. "The irony isn't lost on me. You—Mercy—haven't give me the tongue-lashing I definitely deserved and Grace—Gracie—gave me the second chance I didn't deserve."

A gleam sparkled in Mercy's eyes. "And to think God brought you back into her life right now. You and Gracie and music." She shook her head. "Maybe God has a perfect plan for all of us if we'd just follow his lead."

Where You lead, I will follow.

Yes. God had led him here. To Grace. To Mercy. To complete forgiveness.

And to a new beginning that just might include making guitars and giving lessons alongside the right girl.

While God had used this woman and her redemption story to give him hope for his own family reconciliation.

"Can I give you a hug, future sister?"

"Yes, you may, future brother." Mercy giggled, then stood and opened her arms.

***

Grace parked behind the Way Stop and got out of her car.

Who to talk to first? Dad or Tyler? Dad would be excited beyond belief, but she couldn't risk Tyler walking in on that party and feeling left out. She needed to tell him first.

If only she knew how to open that conversation.

Oh, why had she waited so long to let him know she did more than play the guitar? Or at least dreamed of doing more?

Now more than ever she could sympathize with his hesitancy to go home.

She entered the back door through the kitchen.

First, a little sustenance. For bravery. And then she'd pick a guitar off the wall and ask Tyler to play with her.

Yes. That would be perfect. And if he mentioned her voice or music choice, she could mention her dream... Followed by a "you'll never believe it..."

As she pushed through the kitchen door into the main room, she heard Tyler's voice first. "I am so glad I found you here."

Her eyes darted to the left and the sight of him hugging someone. He faced away from her, but she easily recognized the red-purple hair resting on his shoulder.

Not again.

She ducked back into the kitchen.

Tyler couldn't be hugging her sister. What was next? Kissing under the mistletoe she—they—hung near the tree just yesterday?

Tears blinded her eyes.

Could he have so quickly forgotten her? Or worse, did he really not know the difference between them?

She retraced her steps to the back door and the fresh air outside. No way could she risk running into anyone she knew until her emotions were under control. Which meant her room was off limits.

No. What she needed was a long walk. And an even longer cry.

She tucked her cold hands into her coat pockets and rounded the building. Just down the road was a dirt path that would take her closer to the lake and a usually-calming view. Exactly what she needed.

"Hey, can you help me?" A somewhat familiar voice called from behind her.

She turned to see Tyler outside the Way Stop wearing a black leather coat. And no beard.

Anger replaced her earlier hurt as she stomped his direction. "You finally shaved your beard and stopped hiding for Mercy's sake?"

His puzzled expression was her first—next—clue that she'd yelled at the wrong man. This had to be his twin brother Gavin.

"Does that mean you like beards or not?" His wide smile was followed by a wink. "Because I could be convinced to grow one if that's what the lady prefers."

A month ago, she might have been flattered, but Tyler had since stolen her heart and left every other man lacking in comparison. Even if the man was his musically-talented mirror image.

Mirror image. Like her own twin.

If Tyler heard his brother's words, would he be jealous? Or see it as teasing? Had she misunderstood the scene inside? If she'd stuck around, would she have been relieved or even more broken-hearted?

Gavin's grin faded. "Since you've obviously mistaken me for my brother, I know you've seen Tyler around here." He stepped closer. "If you can just point me in the right direction, we'll get out of your hair. It's time for him to come home."

Her heart cracked open even more. Tyler didn't belong here. He already had a home in Branson with his family.

"I have seen Tyler." She swallowed the lump in her throat at her impending loss. Then instead of pointing at the door behind her and being a personal witness to their brotherly reunion, she gestured toward the road. "He's been staying at his—your—great uncle's fishing cabin. I assume you know how to get there?"

Gavin nodded. "I do. Thank you." He strode toward his car and soon drove out of sight.

She followed at a slower pace while tears streamed down her cheeks. Once she reached the dirt path and relative privacy, she pulled out her phone and texted Tyler that she'd have to take a rain check on their dinner.

As if he'd ever return to Ridgedale.

It was time to let Tyler go. To face her future alone.

But would that solo future include the stage or not? That remained to be seen, because without Tyler, the music in her soul had gone silent.

CANDEE FICK

CHAPTER THIRTEEN

Tyler trudged through the woods. Gracie had never shown up at the Way Stop. He'd have thought that she'd been delayed in town, except he'd seen her parked car when he had finally outstayed his welcome inside.

Had her hair turned into a disaster? Was she embarrassed to face him? Or since they'd made plans for dinner…

He checked his phone. Not only were there no bars, but no power either. How long had his phone been dead?

An uneasy sensation ran down his spine and he picked up the pace. The sooner he got to the cabin and an outlet, the sooner he could check for messages.

Except when he stepped into the clearing, he spotted Gavin's car parked out front beside his truck.

His stomach twisted into a knot. No way to bluff his way out of this unless he could pretend he'd only just arrived in the area. His conscience recoiled at the lie.

Not to mention his twin would see right through any excuse.

The time had come to face the music.

He opened the front door to find Gavin lounged on the couch in front of the blazing fire drinking coffee.

"Ah, there he is. The prodigal son who got lost on his way home."

CANDEE FICK

"How'd you find me?" Tyler shut the door and forced himself to stand still. Even with the sarcasm, he hadn't realized how much he had missed his brother.

"Must have been the twin connection."

"Really?" Others claimed the mysterious bond, but why would it take a month to bring him to his doorstep?

Gavin shrugged. "Actually, I've had a feeling something was wrong every time an episode of *Making Music* aired. Couldn't put my finger on it, but then during Thanksgiving dinner, one of the cousins asked about borrowing your truck for a moving job. Said he'd seen me driving it around town several weeks ago and knew I had the keys." He raised an eyebrow as if hoping Tyler would fill in the gaps.

Instead, Tyler turned away and poured himself a cup of coffee.

Gavin sighed. "Then yesterday, I ran into a friend who asked how the fishing had been in Hollister."

Tyler joined his brother on the couch. "Guess I should be thankful it took several weeks for them to tattle, but why are you here? Why not call?"

"Like you would answer." An exaggerated eye roll reminded Tyler of the lousy cell service and his dead phone.

He pulled it out of his pocket and retreated to the kitchen area again to plug it in.

"Mom said you'd called on her birthday but hasn't heard from you since. None of us have. And when she couldn't reach you for Thanksgiving, it was hard to watch her fake being happy for our sakes."

Tyler winced at the realization he'd been so enamored by Gracie that he'd forgotten what his absence might be costing the others he loved.

"I have no idea what's been going on in your life, but do you know what I think? That you're selfish. When are you going to man up and think about someone else?" Gavin set down his cup and propped his elbows on his knees. "At least come home for Christmas."

86

Tyler sighed and returned to his spot beside his brother. "I almost came home on her birthday."

Gavin went rigid. "You've been in Missouri since then?"

His shoulders slumped and he nodded. "Except I couldn't just show up with a 'Happy Birthday, Mom, from your failure of a son who got used by a girl then dumped the same day his chances at the big time went up in smoke.' Not exactly something I wanted to admit when the rest of you have your lives together."

"Sorry, bro, but nobody who matters cares about that stuff...only about your heart." Gavin nodded at the dust-free, obviously used Bible on the coffee table. "And if you're truly spending time in the Word, you're more than halfway home again."

Tyler squirmed under the hard-hitting truths. "Well, there's not any television here and nothing else to do."

A raised eyebrow cut him off.

He sighed. "You're right. I've read most of the Bible in the last month when not busy—"

"Making a guitar?"

"You saw that?" Tyler glanced through the open bedroom door at the instrument on the bed.

"It's got a quality sound, but is obviously handmade."

"Hey, it was my first attempt. Luke Mitchell helped a lot."

"As in Mitchell's Way Stop down the road?" Gavin elbowed him. "No wonder that cute blonde outside knew you were here at the cabin."

"Blonde? You saw Gracie?" Had Gavin flirted, too? A twinge of jealousy soured in his stomach.

Gavin's expression turned serious. "The Bible, an acoustic guitar, and a nice girl for a change? It's about time you grew up."

Tyler swallowed hard. "So have you, brother. Because I was always the one getting us into trouble and now here you are. Being brave, taking a stand, and speaking the truth. You've changed."

Gavin sighed and leaned back into the lumpy cushions. "I have to admit that it's been good for me to be myself for a few months instead of always part of a pair. But it all started with Gloria."

"She's the one who convinced you to bail on me." He recalled his harsh words toward his twin. Words that were grossly unfair considering that all along his brother had made the right choice to stay in Branson. "Will you forgive me? I was so blinded by ambition that I threw away everything that truly mattered."

"Of course, I forgive you." Gavin blinked several times. "Especially since I know how close I came to doing the same. Gloria might have given me the nudge, but I was the one who had to take that hard walk down the aisle at the theater and rejoin the family. And they were waiting with open arms."

"But that was only after a day. You never actually went to Vegas like I did. And stayed away for months. It might be too late for me." Tears pricked his eyes.

"They're still there waiting for you to return. They—we—have never stopped praying for you."

God had answered those prayers and gotten Tyler's attention in the only way he would have listened. Now, while he longed to be welcomed back, he didn't feel worthy of a second chance. Didn't feel worthy to be a son or brother again.

Gavin must have noticed his expression because he reached over and rested a hand on Tyler's shoulder. "You don't have to meet the whole gang the first day. Just make things right with Mom and Dad to start. In fact, you can camp out in my spare bedroom for a few days. I could invite them over tonight after the show or make arrangements for a small family lunch after church tomorrow instead."

Baby steps. First his brother, then his parents. Followed by the rest?

Tyler nodded, then reached to hug his brother. "Thank you."

Gavin slapped him on the back. "You're welcome."

A burden lifted from his shoulders. With his twin's forgiveness and invitation, he was well on his way home. And no time like the present to finish his journey.

Surely Grace would understand if he needed to reschedule their date.

"It won't take me long to pack, but I need a few hours to wrap things up here and then I'll be home."

Home. No sweeter word in the English language.

***

A couple hours after Gavin left, Tyler tossed his overnight bag onto the passenger side floorboards in the cab of his truck. His bulging suitcase from the trip to Las Vegas and the two boxes he'd pulled out of storage several weeks before were already loaded into the back.

And his new guitar was carefully strapped in with the seatbelt until he could get his padded case out of storage.

He took a deep breath and one more long look at the cabin that had been his refuge while God transformed his heart. The pipes and plumbing had been winterized again so nothing could freeze and with the door locked and key hidden in the usual spot, there was only one thing still to do.

Tyler sighed, then slid behind the wheel. A few minutes later, he parked beside the Way Stop.

In the gloom of gathering storm clouds, lights gleamed from the workshop's windows.

Might as well start with the easy goodbye first.

He knocked, then opened the door and slipped inside. As expected, Luke was busy sanding what appeared to be a guitar neck, but across the workbench, Gracie sat with her head in her hands.

"Sorry to interrupt."

She lifted her head and his heart sank to see the evidence of tears on her face.

Her father glanced between the two of them. "Come to say goodbye, have you?"

Tyler blinked. "How did you—"

The man nodded at his daughter. "Heard your brother stopped by earlier. Knew it was just a matter of time anyway."

Tyler sank onto a stool and picked up sandpaper and another piece of wood. He needed something to do with his hands. "It's not really goodbye, but I did close up the cabin and am heading to Branson tonight. I'll be staying with my brother for a few days." He tried to capture Gracie's eyes, but she busied herself cleaning sawdust off the workspace and avoiding his gaze.

"As Gavin reminded me, it's long past time I cleared the air with my family. But thanks to both of you, I'm in a much better position than before."

"How's that?" Luke paused his sanding motions.

"True Light. True Faith."

"And...?"

"I don't need the spotlight or the attention. I know who I am and whose I am. But I'm not sure I ever want to step onto a stage again."

"Why not?" Gracie's voice cracked as she finally entered the conversation.

"Without good accountability, I'm afraid I might get sucked back into my old habits." He turned his attention to his mentor. "How can I balance fame with my faith?"

"Do you remember what I said several weeks ago when you first wandered in here?"

His mind spun trying to recall that first conversation, but too many talks had happened since then. "No, sir."

"I believe I may have said something about being an instrument in the hands of the Master Craftsman."

He smiled. "You did. And then taught me all about making a guitar."

Luke dropped his sandpaper and folded his arms over his chest. "We are all instruments with unique sounds. All designed for specific notes in different settings. Some from a stage. Others in church. And even a few in a classroom or teaching sea gulls to find the tune. Now, together we make a symphony that sings God's praises, but individually we all have a part to play. And it's our responsibility to obey that call."

"So, I'm supposed to play my guitar?"

"Probably." Luke chuckled. "That's something you'll have to ask the Master about, but I truly believe you can use music to point others to God." His gaze shifted to include his daughter. "There are always those who get side-tracked by misguided ambition but just like the apostle Paul's life changed after encountering Jesus and the prodigal was welcomed home by his father, there are new chapters to be written. New songs to be sung."

"You can stop with the riddles and metaphors, Dad." Gracie rolled her eyes.

Tyler smirked. She certainly had a way of not putting up with any nonsense.

"You want it in plain English? God's gifts of music are made to be used, not to be hidden away in the backwoods. If He gave you a gift, use it. Period. End of story."

"My Granny always said the same thing." Tyler shifted on the metal stool. "That we were to use God's gifts wherever they took us."

And his were currently taking him home and away from Gracie.

If only that didn't scare him so much.

***

Grace winced as her dad's words found their mark.

God had given her the gifts of music and lyrics and now the gift of an open door to Nashville and the world of performing. It was up to her to use those gifts for God's glory wherever they took her.

Of course, Tyler thought the lecture was meant for him. And perhaps it was. Except that before he had walked in, she and her dad had been in the middle of a very honest conversation about her options and all of her fears.

Including those revolving around the too handsome fellow musician in the room.

Tyler cleared his throat. "Luke, I just wanted to say thanks again for being used by God to point me in the right direction. All of our talks over the past few weeks have made a huge difference. And maybe with God's help and accountability like that from my very-blunt brother, I can stay on the right path this time."

"Sounds like a good plan."

Tyler checked his watch. "That's assuming this prodigal ever gets back to town and has that overdue talk with his parents." His attempt at a joke fell flat along with a smile that didn't quite reach his eyes.

In fact, he looked truly petrified to face his family and admit his mistakes. While she'd been consumed with worries about their relationship or lack thereof, he had other issues on his mind.

Dad stood and pulled Tyler into a back-slapping man embrace. "I'll be praying for you, son."

Tyler closed his eyes for a moment as a smile flitted across his lips. "I need it."

He seemed so relieved she couldn't help but offer the same. "You'll be in my prayers, too." After all, no matter what her future held, chances were she wouldn't forget him any time soon.

His eyes snapped open and found hers. "I'll call you and we'll do dinner soon."

Her heart didn't want to hope but emotion clogged her throat. Leaving her no option but to simply nod.

A few moments later, the door clicked shut behind him. She listened for the sound of a truck engine revving to life and braced herself as it faded into the distance.

He was truly gone.

She stifled a sob.

"When are you going to tell him about your offer?"

"I was going to today. Until I saw him with—"

Dad frowned. "She told you what really happened, right?"

Grace nodded, still feeling foolish at her internal over-reaction. "But then his brother showed up and I knew he didn't belong here."

"Not any more than you do."

She winced. They'd been over this argument several times already this afternoon, not to mention the day he revealed he had sent her demo tape to a friend.

"Home is a nest. A safety net. Not a hammock or hideaway."

"I know." She swallowed hard. "But I'm afraid to fly." Especially if that meant flying alone.

He nodded toward the stack of brochures he included with every instrument he made. A brochure that told the story of Ed Stilley and the guitar that started it all. "Like Tyler etched on his guitar as a reminder, all you need is to have faith in God."

"I'm trying." If only she didn't feel so incredibly unsettled about her future. About Tyler. About whether or not she could step into the spotlight without getting sick.

Even after hours spent wandering and crying and praying, she was no closer to an answer to what to do about Tyler or her future. And the current headache accumulated as a result of that cryfest wasn't helping matters.

Perhaps things would be clearer tomorrow.

Grace sighed. "I'm going to go help Mercy with supper."

Dad picked up his sandpaper again. "I'll be there in a bit once I finish this piece."

Her lips curved into a smile. "Famous last words, Dad."

He shrugged. "I do my best praying while working."

She could use those prayers. And so could Tyler.

Grace donned her coat and then slipped out the door, turning toward their two-story house next door. Which reminded her that miles away, a prodigal son had turned his own corner toward home.

Lord, please make his path straight.

And bring him back so I can tell him I'm leaving.

With another sob, Grace hurried on through the cold.

CHAPTER FOURTEEN

Tyler's stomach revolted at the smell of the take-out food his siblings, their spouses, and the kids were piling onto plates. Perched on the edge of his parents' couch, he rubbed sweaty hands on his knees.

Dad stopped beside him and addressed the room. "Once everyone has something to eat, gather round. Tyler's already talked to your mom and I this morning, but wanted to talk to everyone else at the same time. Thanks for changing your plans so we could gather as a family."

The earlier chatter quickly died down and soon every available inch of floor space in the combination living room and dining room was occupied. Tyler found himself squeezed in between Gavin and their father on the couch.

Their unspoken support meant the world. Over in the kitchen his mom was consolidating the empty containers for the trash and he caught her watery smile.

That tear-filled reunion and meandering explanation had been difficult. Hopefully it was easier the second time around.

He cleared his throat. "I'm going to tell it all from the beginning and then answer any questions you have. You might have seen a few episodes along the way, but despite my now breaking the non-disclosure agreement not to reveal the outcome of the show, I wanted to let you know before the rest of the world finds out that Wednesday's episode will end with us—me—being eliminated from the competition."

A few of them reacted to the news. Joy gasped and Nick frowned, as if sad on his behalf. But his oldest brother, Matt, just shook his head. "Sorry, bro, but I guess I'm not surprised since you're here in Missouri...and don't seem very happy about it."

Tyler's shoulders relaxed. "I wasn't happy then either. But mostly because of something that probably won't be included in the edited version of the show. Truth is that while walking off some extra energy and pre-show jitters, I accidentally learned we were going to get cut several hours before our performance...when I overheard Brittany making a deal with one of the judges. Our group's mentor." He glanced toward the kids in the room and censored his words. "A moving into his suite and becoming his next star kind of deal."

There were definitely more reactions to that revelation.

He stared at his folded hands. "And since I'm the one who took her—followed her—to Vegas in the first place, I should have known what she was capable of. Now, I know that getting dumped by my girlfriend and cut from the show isn't exactly the same as the prodigal son slopping pigs, but it was still hard to swallow the fact I'm a failed musician who trusted the wrong people and threw away what really mattered in the process." He made eye contact with those he had left behind. "I was embarrassed to admit my mistakes and have been hiding out ever since."

A few feet away, Nick's fiancée Gloria nudged Tyler's foot with her own. "Hey. I've been there at rock bottom myself. My trip started by face planting into a mop bucket."

An unexpected burst of laughter escaped his lips. The memory of seeing the glamorous woman sprawled on the concrete floor backstage at The Sherwood Theater broke the tension.

Gloria laughed along with Nick and Gavin who had also been there to witness her fall, then she shrugged. "But at least your downfall wasn't tabloid worthy like my dad's issues. Or Brittany's recent scandals."

"What are you talking about?" He glanced around the room at the mixture of eye-rolls and disgusted expressions. "Hey, somebody fill me in. I've been avoiding social media for weeks."

His youngest sister Robin took pity on him with a brief summary of a drunken argument with the wife of a professional athlete at a casino. And the whole thing had been caught on video and gone viral. Apparently, Brittany now had a vocal opposition armed with a hashtag who hoped Tyler's group would get eliminated so she would finally stop flaunting herself and calling in favors around town.

Tyler shook his head. "They say there's no such thing as bad publicity, but I don't think that will help her chances at keeping the recording contract I overheard them discussing."

"Don't know. Don't care." Nick shrugged. "But if you were eliminated weeks ago, what have you been doing since then?"

"Hiding." Tyler rubbed his beard and all of his brothers laughed. "Camping out at Uncle Joshua's cabin. Eating awful canned soup every day. Chopping wood to stay warm. Reading the Bible cover to cover. Getting right with God again. Building a guitar from scratch."

"A guitar? You?" John, the baby of the family, snorted. "You never were very good with tools."

Tyler raised an eyebrow. "Well, I had a very patient teacher. Luke Mitchell makes a—"

"Mitchell, you say?" Matt looked thoughtful. "He's got quite the reputation for quality workmanship."

"And a pretty daughter." Gavin jabbed an elbow into Tyler's ribs. "Gonna tell them about Grace?"

Heat rose in his face. "Yes, I met a girl. The girl." He grinned as he thought of another way to break the remaining ice. "Actually, I was about to come home weeks ago, but when Mom started telling me about how everyone was busy expanding the family with more kids…" He nodded at Matt and his wife Mary, then Joy and her husband Tom. "And saying 'I do.'" He found his sister Robin snuggled into her new husband's arms and his smile grew. "And getting engaged…" He nudged Nick's foot and winked at Gloria. "And dating…" He returned the elbow jab to Gavin and tilted his head toward John.

Tyler paused, then sighed dramatically. "I guess I felt left out and couldn't come home until I found a girl, too. And Gracie is most definitely a keeper."

The explosion of overlapping conversation and questions and laughter swept the remaining tension from the room.

"Now you know where I've been and what's been going on. But before I get truly caught up on the rest of all *your* news, I just have to say I'm sorry I left the way I did. I'm sorry I thought more about my ambition than the problems I was causing for you. And sorry for all the years of drifting away from our foundation of faith." He swallowed the lump in his throat and asked the important question. "Will you forgive me for not being the brother you needed?"

Their overwhelming—and unanimous—response smothered him in a wave of unconditional love and forgiveness. And then attention finally turned to the food and the normal conversations of a large multi-generational family gathered a few weeks before Christmas.

His mom brought him a plate and he was finally able to eat. Then sinking back into the couch cushions, he soaked up the atmosphere of the family rooms above the Sherwood Hotel. Of course, Mom had already decorated for Christmas in her day-after-Thanksgiving tradition. And somewhere in the background, classic tunes played on the stereo.

A few weeks ago, he hadn't been sure it was possible. But somehow, with God's grace, he was truly home again.

However, as he eavesdropped on the conversations around him, he caught several mentions of a lineup for their singalong night.

He leaned toward Gavin and lowered his voice. "What's this about singing along? When did that start?"

Gavin narrowed his eyes. "When you left. They—we—had to fill the gaps in the schedule where the Rockin' show had been." He went on to explain how the informal singalong nights and back-to-back weekend shows had kept the tourists happy but had taken a toll on them all. But there would be new artists filling blocks at the theater starting in January so the Sherwood show would be revamping and cutting back to allow for more family time.

It made sense for the newlyweds and those with infants to readjust their priorities for a season, but where did that leave him?

"Hey, Tyler." John plopped onto the carpet by his feet. "Since you're back, do you want to do a special number with me for the Christmas show?"

He hesitated. "I'm not sure what I'll be doing." Or if it was wise for him to step onto another stage so soon.

His non-answer landed him in the hot seat and soon Matt, Nick, and Dad had circled around them. Matt took the lead. "Like in the past, the special show will have a few trademark sets from our main program, but this year, we're also adding plenty of Christmas medley's and singalong caroling for a feel-good evening for the audience. We could use you as much as you're willing to participate."

Nick nodded. "Of course, there would be rehearsals, but the biggest commitment is Friday and Saturday nights two weekends in a row."

Tyler set his empty plate aside. "Let me think about it. Because I'm not sure I want to be in the spotlight for a while."

John snorted. "You? Don't want attention?"

Both Nick and Matt laughed, but at least Dad and Gavin seemed more thoughtful than confused.

"I'm serious. That's what turned my head and then my heart in the first place. I'm not sure I trust myself to be onstage with a microphone, at least not as a soloist. Maybe I would be fine in a group or doing backup, but I don't know." He looked down at his hands and tried to put his thoughts into words. "What I *do* know is that I love music and that I'll definitely be doing something musical in the future. Or at least be around it like Nick's backstage stuff. Or maybe even play in a band instead of singing. Because I'd forgotten how much I love playing the guitar, especially acoustic."

Wide eyes met his declaration and he rubbed a hand over his beard. While it should be clear to them that he'd had a heart change, he wasn't going to make a decision about performing without asking God first.

He shifted his gaze from person to person before landing on his father. "Honestly, I've been praying for direction for a few weeks, but I don't feel a peace about coming back full time. It's almost like there's something else out there for me to do. To be." His voice trailed off.

Where You lead, I will follow.

God, show me where to go.

Dad coughed. "I believe with all my heart that God has a plan for your life and your gifts. We'll be praying for you to find that path, son."

An hour later, he still carried the inner warmth of his family's reception. But instead of heading back to Gavin's apartment for the afternoon, Tyler made a right turn instead.

He couldn't wait to tell Gracie about what had happened.

CHAPTER FIFTEEN

After they'd returned from church, Grace had retreated to her bedroom for some peace and quiet away from her energetic nephew and his never-ending questions. And while Dad's frown made it clear he wanted to talk more about her options, he had gifted her with space instead of insisting she join them for the noon meal.

Between yesterday's phone call from Nashville and Tyler's departure, she had a lot on her mind. A lot to pray about and a desperate need for that still small voice.

Once behind closed doors, she quickly changed into her favorite green sweater and a well-worn pair of jeans, then curled up in the overstuffed chair and stared out the window.

Beyond the glass and between the tree tops, she caught a glimpse of water. And somewhere between her perch and Table Rock Lake was an empty fishing cabin.

Oh, how she missed Tyler. His smile. His teasing. And yes, his kisses that warmed her heart and resurrected her romantic dreams.

However, despite all their encounters at the Way Stop and her dad's workshop, they'd never actually gone anywhere in public including to church. Would their relationship ever step out of the shadows of privacy? Could it change for the better or would going public only spotlight their differences?

Then again, she'd know those answers soon enough since his journey home involved a huge step out of hiding. Especially with the size of his family and the awkwardly difficult subject of how his time in Vegas had ended.

God, I assume he's already talked to some of his family. If it didn't go well, please comfort him. Remind him of who he is in You. And if it went better than expected...

Her breath caught in her lungs before she blew it out slowly.

If Your will is for him to perform with his family again, make his path clear.

Even if that path led them apart.

Would she have the chance to share her dreams with him? To brainstorm the possibilities? Or was it too late for them? Had their lives only been meant to intersect for a few wonderful weeks?

Restless and fidgety, she reached for her guitar and began to strum. Like in years gone by, something about holding the instrument in her hands allowed her tangled thoughts to unravel into pure notes.

What if Tyler's journey home meant he stayed there and she never saw him again?

Where did that leave her? In a classroom somewhere? Serving coffee at the Way Stop? Or moving to Nashville?

God, where am I supposed to go? What am I to do?

As her fingers drifted over the strings and familiar melodies emerged, part of the answer grew crystal clear.

Music was her lifeblood. Her gift. And her future.

Because denying God's gift and hiding that light in the backwoods wasn't an option anymore. Like Tyler's Granny had taught her children...and like Dad had reminded Tyler of yesterday when she'd accidentally intruded on their goodbye and missed out on her own...God's gifts were made to be used.

Teaching had never been her calling.

First thing tomorrow morning, she'd withdraw her application from consideration by the local school district.

With that decision made, a burden she hadn't realized she'd been carrying lifted from her shoulders and was replaced by a fresh joy and freedom. In response, she ducked her head toward the strings and swayed along with the notes flowing from beneath her fingers.

No doubt about it, she was supposed to pursue the music and the message God had placed on her heart for as long as the door was open. And if that door led her to a stage and national tour, well, she'd do it.

Somehow.

While relying on God's strength alone.

But while opportunity knocked, it was up to her to answer.

She sighed and reached for her phone. Like he'd said, she didn't have to sign the specific deal being offered, but she could at least get more information about the process and the industry.

Before she could change her mind, she scrolled through her recent calls for the number and dialed. Three rings later, Mr. Brent answered. "Richard here."

"Uh, yes, this is Grace Mitchell. And I—"

"Great to hear from you. Did Christmas come early? Am I getting on a plane tomorrow?" The excitement in his voice made her smile.

"I don't know about Christmas, but I'd definitely like to meet." She blew out a breath and laughed to herself. "Like you said, I have a lot of questions."

"Of course." His tone switched to all business. "I'll do my best to answer them all so you can make the best decision for you. Who else will be joining us?"

"My dad for sure." '

"I'd expect no less. However, since you live so close to Branson, if you happen to know anyone in the music industry there, you're more than welcome to bring a friend as well. I have a feeling that an objective opinion from someone who knows the business might help ease your concerns."

"That's true." Because she definitely had plenty of concerns. Yet the only performer she personally knew was

Tyler. And while she would love to have his input, inviting him along meant she had finally revealed her secret…and that he'd forgiven her for hiding so much. She swallowed hard. "I'll keep that in mind."

After confirming the location and time, she disconnected the call and tossed her phone onto the bed.

Ready or not, Tuesday would change the course of her life. And even though her stomach floated like she was perched atop the highest of high dives, there was also immense relief to have taken that first step.

While God alone knew where the road ahead might take her, all she had to think about was the next step. Her smile grew.

One step at a time.

But what was next?

Actually, now that the appointment was made, her next step should be to revisit the songs on her demo tape since it had been a long time since she had played a few of them.

With new energy, she opened her laptop on the nearby desk and pulled up the old files containing her background tracks. After a quick tune to synchronize the sounds, she sang along to the mixture of live guitar and recorded bass and drum lines.

Her mind soon spun with ideas to update and improve the sound, and it wasn't long before she lost herself in the music as one song merged into the next.

Where You lead me, I will follow.

***

Tyler knocked on the front door of the Mitchell's two-story home, then glanced at Gracie's car sitting alongside the other family cars. Inside, he heard a child's squeal followed by pounding feet.

Then Luke opened the door with a cute light-haired imp attached to his knee. "Hi, Tyler. Wasn't sure I'd see you again this soon. Things work out okay at home?"

"They did." He smiled, but no place seemed as much like home as here. "Is Gracie here?"

After a momentary pause, Luke nodded, then stepped backward inviting him inside. "Can I trust you with her heart? Her dreams?"

Tyler blinked. That was both blunt and direct, but the answer was easy. "With God's help, I will do my best." Okay. That sounded lame.

But it must have been close enough to the right answer because Luke smirked. "I'll take your coat." The man waved a hand toward the stairs. "Then first door on the right. Just follow the music."

Follow the...

Once he knew to listen, he could make out a few notes from a guitar above the retreating steps of the obviously-bored child. Mercy poked her head around the corner in time to catch her son.

Which meant Gracie was the one playing.

Should he detour to his truck to get his own guitar? No. There would time enough for that later. Right now, he couldn't wait to see how much they had in common when it came to music.

"Thank you." Tyler finally shrugged out of his coat and handed it over before taking the stairs two at a time.

At the top landing, he could not only hear the music but also the voice. That amazing voice from the workshop. Luke's student who was going to be a star. No wonder the man wanted to know Tyler would support her dreams.

He stepped closer.

"Where You lead me, I will follow."

He smiled at the confirmation that God had led him to Gracie after all then tapped on the closed door.

The singing stopped. "Come in."

Tyler turned the knob and swung the door open. Gracie was seated cross-legged on an upholstered chair with a battered guitar on her lap and an open laptop on the writing desk nearby. She glanced up and her eyes widened. She quickly reached over to click the mouse on her computer and the synthesized drum beat stopped.

This was awkward, and yet it was up to him to open the conversation.

He folded his arms over his chest and leaned against the door frame with a smile. "I've been meaning to ask if you wanted to play with me some time."

She giggled and relaxed back in her chair. "Me, too. Except I kept getting distracted by other things." A rosy blush covered her cheeks as if she too remembered how most conversations lately had ended with kisses. "Come on in."

Since the only spot available was on the bed, he left the door wide open to remove any temptation, then sat on the burgundy-patterned quilt.

She glanced from the open door back to him. "How did it go with your parents?"

He gave her the quick version of the conversations and his welcome home. "Funny thing is, it wasn't nearly as hard as I thought it would be. I guess the longer I held onto the secret and delayed telling, the bigger it got in my mind."

"I know all about secrets." She lifted the guitar. "You once asked if I still play and I'd been meaning to bring that subject up again."

"But you don't just play, you also sing." He nodded toward her computer. "And arrange."

"How did you—"

"Your dad played your music in the workshop one day. Said you were a student who was going to be a star."

Her face whitened. "There's more truth there than he knew at the time."

Tyler willed himself to be patient. "Will you tell me?"

She swallowed hard, then stared at the wall behind him as she told the story of a broken-hearted high school student devoting her time to learning the guitar to drown her sorrow and eventually becoming a stereotypical band nerd with multiple instruments and of going on to college to pursue a degree in musical performance.

She shook her head. "I had this dream of singing my own music someday. But then I faced the competition from my talented classmates. The constant comparisons. The stage fright. The nit-picking of technique by my professors and peers. The criticism that guitar wasn't a sophisticated instrument." She shuddered. "And then I remembered from high school how fame could change a person's personality and worried that if I pursued that path, I might end up blind to God's leading."

He squirmed at the knowledge that he'd unknowingly influenced her life in more ways than one.

"I'm glad I learned enough from my vocal coach to protect my voice in the long term, but I was more-than-happy to switch my focus to music production instead. I thought I could still be around music without needing to be in the spotlight." She nodded toward her laptop. "Producing one song for a class project turned into an addicting side hobby until I had enough songs to fill an album. Except little by little my insecurities kept rising up and I let fear swallow up my dream. I decided to play it safe and double-majored in music education."

Education? Like a teacher? Or choir director? He bit his lip and studied her appearance. Even with the new highlights in her hair and makeup that accented the brilliant green of her eyes brought out by the matching color of her sweater, he had a hard time picturing her in anything but jeans.

"What's that look for?

"Sorry, I'm having a hard time imagining you as a teacher, especially after seeing you as a waitress so often. And now after hearing your equally beautiful voice." She squirmed under his assessment, so he went for the deflection. "The song you were singing when I got here, is that an original or a cover?"

"Original." The word came out in a whisper.

"Wow. Gracie, you are extremely gifted. I've been singing and playing for years, but have never managed to write a single song, let alone one so compelling. I haven't been able to get those lyrics out of my head since I heard them and I have a feeling others won't either." He leaned forward and propped his elbows on his thighs. "What are you doing to get your music out into the world?"

"Funny you should ask that." She set her guitar aside and folded her arms around her bent knees. "A few days before you showed up in our neck of the woods, Dad decided I needed a push from the family nest and sent my songs to a friend who gave it to a friend…"

"And?"

"And yesterday morning I got a call from the head of Brent-Hill Records who's flying here to talk to me about a multi-album deal and a national tour. And I'm out of my league and in over my head and scared spitless at the thought but know I have to at least meet—"

"Breathe, Gracie." Tyler took a deep breath himself at the realization that she had been offered stardom on a platter and didn't want it. Or at least was wise enough not to jump too soon.

She lifted wide eyes brimming with tears. "I've written music. Performed in my bedroom. Arranged multiple tracks on my computer. But I've never, ever, ever sung in front of people outside my college classes and that was never on a stage. With lights. And microphones. I'm going to completely embarrass myself. Surely God doesn't want that, does He?"

He moved to kneel beside her chair and grasped her hand. *God, help me know what wisdom to offer her.*

"You won't be doing this alone. First step, meet with the guy and learn what he expects. How soon you'd perform. How many songs. That sort of thing."

"Will you come with me? Help me ask the right questions?"

"I will." Except he didn't know nearly as much as his parents did about the industry. "If it's okay with you, I can see if my mom is also willing to meet with you. She could give you another perspective."

She squeezed his hand in return. "Please. She's also welcome at the meeting with Mr. Brent."

"I'll see what I can do." A deep peace settled around his shoulders as he embraced the supportive role of adviser. Almost as if his past experiences singing at the Sherwood Theater were meant to prepare him for this.

A sudden flash of insight brought a smile to his face. "And I have an idea for how to get my girlfriend a little low-pressure stage experience too."

CANDEE FICK

CHAPTER SIXTEEN

On a Friday night almost three weeks later, Grace stood backstage at the Sherwood Theater peeking out the curtains at the rapidly-filling auditorium.

Sooner than she thought possible, she would take the stage as a guest artist with the Sherwoods as part of their Christmas concert. It wasn't the medley of carols she'd sing as part of an ensemble that had her so nervous.

No. Looming on the schedule was the spotlight where she would sing two of her own songs.

Alone.

She pressed a hand over her tumbling stomach beneath the festive red sweater. Could she really do it?

Tyler and his family believed in her. And so did Richard Brent.

Her mind flashed back to that fateful meeting at the Way Stop where she'd been flanked by her dad and Tyler with his mother by his side. The head of the recording company had been slightly impressed that she was dating one of the *Making Music* artists and quickly acknowledged Patricia Sherwood's experience.

Grace's musical potential had risen by association.

Except, after a detailed explanation of what the next year would hold, her biggest—only real—objection to the deal had been ruthlessly exposed.

Then Tyler had proposed a way for her to get some stage experience before the deal was finalized. He'd argued it would be good for the record company to know she could deliver, but the warmth in his eyes and the squeeze of his hand under the table had made it clear he was doing it for her.

To build her confidence with a baby step in relative safety and anonymity.

She'd signed the contract and dated it for January 1st, thereby giving her the opportunity to sing her songs before the contract went into effect and the rights to her music could be debated.

And the music mogul had agreed that if for some reason tonight and the next few concerts were a total flop, she could retract without any repercussions.

Since that meeting, it had been a whirlwind of rehearsals with the Sherwood family until she could almost perform her part in their show with her eyes closed. Their support had been a true God-sent blessing. Because in addition to the unspoken welcome to the family as Tyler's girlfriend, their genuine compliments of her music had built her confidence. Of course, they'd been quick to remind her there would always be critics, but all she had to do was remember that God was the only Audience she had to sing for.

Assuming she could survive the night, after a few weekends on this stage, she shouldn't be intimidated by the performance logistics of microphones and lights anymore. Except once she was on tour, she'd be truly alone.

She closed her eyes and tried to imagine herself stepping onto a different stage.

Except her stomach threatened to revolt again.

God, if only I could take them all with me.

Warm hands settled on her shoulders. "Breathe, Gracie."

She turned to face Tyler and looked up into his laughing eyes. "How do you always know what I need?"

"Because I've been there. Here." He nodded over her shoulder at the stage. "I may have started young, but I can still remember the feeling. And then not too long ago, I had the added pressure of television cameras."

"Not helping, Tyler."

He pulled her into his arms. "Remember how you were afraid you'd get blinded by the lights? Well, consider this nervous feeling God's way of keeping you dependent on Him."

Oh, how true that was. *God, You're going to help me tonight, right?*

"And...you're not doing this alone."

"Except for my solo slot."

He shook his head. "Even then, you're not alone. We're still here. I'm still here."

At his declaration, she became increasingly aware of his arms around her and his lips so close to her own. A peace filtered into her heart.

If only Tyler could be with her on the road. Would he be willing to consider the possibility?

"And, I've also learned that when I'm nervous, distractions help." His gaze dipped to her mouth. "Like now."

A moment later, all thoughts of the stage disappeared in the heat of his kiss.

***

Tyler reined in his passion and after a second—gentler—kiss, he lifted his head. With her hands around his neck and playing with his hair, it was clear he'd succeeded in distracting Grace from her nerves. At least for now.

But he still had an important question to ask.

And there was no time like the present.

"Grace? I'm already dreading the distance when you move to Nashville. But I was serious. When you go on tour, you don't have to do that alone." He grasped her hands in his, then after taking a deep breath, slipped to one knee.

Her eyes widened and behind him, someone gasped.

"I can't bear the thought of us being apart. Gracie? Will you…let me carry your guitar?"

She blinked.

"Refill your water bottle?"

A smile flitted around her lips and his nerves eased. "Be part of your road crew? Go with you and keep the hoards of admiring fans at bay? Serve you." *Love you?*

Tears filled her eyes and then she slowly shook her head.

What? No. That was the wrong answer. His breath caught in his throat.

She tugged him to his feet. "You can't be a mere roadie. I need you much closer than that." Her hands slid to his chest and his heart started beating again.

Her voice lowered and her eyes warmed as she raised one hand to stroke his beard. "Will you lead my band? Play the guitar for me? Go to Nashville after Christmas to record the album with me?"

"I'll do whatever you want." A smile tugged at his lips.

"Love me like I love you?" Her voice dropped to a raspy whisper.

"Always." He sealed the declaration with another kiss, then remembered the lyrics to the new song she planned to sing in less than an hour. "I promise you a lifetime of devotion."

Her smile grew and she began to sing along. "I promise you the best of me."

EPILOGUE

One Year Later

Gracie adjusted the fit of the headset microphone around her ears, then fluffed her hair to cover the supports until only the extension along her cheek was visible. A quick pat near her lower back confirmed that the cord was still secure beneath her clothing and connected to the wireless transmitter at her waist.

Bejeweled button-up blouses and strappy heels were her only concessions to onstage fashion even if the embroidery on the pockets of her jeans was still several steps fancier than her waitressing norm. But the semi-casual look helped keep the audience's focus on the lyrics instead of her appearance.

And as the tour for her debut album wound to a close, rumors of a Dove nomination and negotiations for another tour with higher profile venues proved that her message had found an audience. Which made recording her second album after the first of the year an added blessing. Living this dream was even sweeter than she'd imagined.

God, thank You once again for answered prayers. Especially for Tyler.

She glanced at the band where they'd gathered nearby for a few last minute instructions and reminders from their fearless leader. As if the past months playing together on the road hadn't solidified the group.

And her relationship with Tyler.

Because, as promised, he'd been there every step of the way. Not just in the band but as a constant source of accountability even before he'd become her manager.

And then the night before they left Nashville on tour, he'd once again dropped to one knee with a very different question.

She admired the sparkling diamond on her left hand and grinned. One last concert tonight and then they'd be headed home for Christmas. And their wedding.

"Ready, Gracie?" Her fiancé rested warm hands on her shoulders.

"I am."

"Promise?" He quirked one eyebrow in the flirty move that had become theirs alone. A move that reminded her of the lyrics to her number one single.

"I do." She eased up onto her toes and gave him a quick kiss. Followed by a slower one that brought Tyler's arms around her waist.

Her stage name might stay the same, but she couldn't wait to become Mrs. Sherwood.

The venue's stage manager cleared his throat nearby. "Show time, Miss Mitchell."

Right. The reason she was here.

Tyler stepped back with a cocky grin, then followed the band onto the stage while she strapped on her own guitar, a gift from her father to commemorate the release of her first album.

Onstage, she saw Tyler rub a finger along the neck of his instrument and the engraved words she knew were there.

He looked her way and they shared a smile. He winked and she blew him a kiss. Flirting had never been so fun. But after one last Elvis lip curl just for her, he nodded to the drummer to tap out the beat.

And Gracie stepped onto the stage and into the lights, more than ready to sing the songs that would point the audience to the True Light.

CANDEE FICK

DEAR READER

I truly enjoyed the journey of bringing Tyler home and wrapping up the Wardrobe series.

When I sat down to brainstorm this particular story, I had no idea where my research would lead. With a vague idea that it might be good to bring Tyler back in touch with the rustic foundations of his music, I did an online search for homemade instruments in the Ozarks. Near the top of the results was a story about Ed Stilley, and suddenly I'd found both the perfect message and symbol to trigger Tyler's journey home to faith and family and singing again. Yes, Mr. Stilley really did make and give away several hundred instruments to children and yes, they really were inscribed with the words "True Light. True Faith. Have Faith in God." I love it when my research adds unexpected—perhaps even God-ordained—depth to my stories.

As I send this particular book to print, I can't help but think of how the entire series wrestled with the issue of fame both at The Wardrobe Dinner Theater in Fort Collins and at the Sherwood Theater in Branson. Because of the nature of those businesses, every character in each story (heroes, heroines, sidekicks, cast members, band, and villains) had to come to some sort of conclusion.

Would they be twisted by or consumed with the pursuit of the spotlight...or do everything they could to avoid the notoriety...or would they find a healthy balance of using God's gifts and talents for an Audience of One?

When I first starting writing *Dance Over Me*, the title and core message were pulled from Zephaniah 3:17. "The Lord your God is with you, he is mighty to save. He will take great delight in you, he will quiet you with his love, he will rejoice over you with singing."

Then, along the way, my characters also kept landing on Jeremiah 29:11 as a secondary theme. "This is God's Word on the subject: 'As soon as Babylon's seventy years are up and not a day before, I'll show up and take care of you as I promised and bring you back home. I know what I'm doing. I have it all planned out—plans to take care of you, not abandon you, plans to give you the future you hope for. When you call on me, when you come and pray to me, I'll listen." (Jeremiah 29:10-12 The Message)

And so, dear reader, I want to leave you with this thought: God truly loves you and has a wonderful plan for your life. And whether you live in or out of the spotlight, He's in the audience and longs to give you a standing ovation. To say "well done, good and faithful servant."

If you're interested in what's next from me, I'm currently working on more titles for the Within the Castle Gates series. With a mixture of historical and contemporary settings planned, each standalone romance features a castle and a heroine struggling to embrace her true identity as a child of God.

If you think others would enjoy this story, please do me a huge favor and leave an honest review at your favorite retailers. A review doesn't have to be more than a few words, but it truly helps others find my books!

And if you'd like to receive monthly email updates about upcoming releases, special deals, and other fun stuff, you can sign up on my website at https://CandeeFick.com.

Thanks again for spending time with one of my books. Happy reading everyone!

MORE BOOKS BY CANDEE FICK

Standalone Fiction

Catch of a Lifetime

The Wardrobe Series

Dance Over Me
Focus On Love
Sing a New Song
A Picture Perfect Christmas
Home For Christmas

Within the Castle Gates Series

Stepping Into the Light
To Win Her Heart
The Lost Heir
Finding Home
Saving Grace
A Castle in the Clouds

Non-Fiction

The Author Toolbox: Practical Tools to Build a Book, a
Platform, a Business, and a Career
Pigskin Parables: Exploring Faith and Football
Pigskin Parables: Devotions from the Game of Football
Making Lemonade: Parents Transforming Special Needs
Devotions from the Garden: Inspiration for Life
Be Like a Tree: The Keys to a Fruitful Life

PREVIEW
STEPPING INTO THE LIGHT

Within the Castle Gates series, Book 1

Sometimes the most heroic live in plain sight.

Tragedy stalks the Gunn castle, most recently when the heir to the Gunn chiefdom died leaving their land vulnerable to attack. But security has come in the promise of a marriage alliance with Clan Sinclair, their powerful neighbors to the north.

The search is on to gather the eligible maidens...except mysterious accidents befall all who join the laird's widow at the castle. Meanwhile, messengers have been spotted along their southern border and Clan Sinclair may be walking into a trap.

With war looming and a madwoman in their midst, the only hope for a peaceful future may lie in the hands of a disfigured Gunn recluse and the overlooked second son of Clan Sinclair.

* * * * *

PROLOGUE

1412 ~ Scottish Highlands

Alone at last, Moira Gunn collapsed to her knees in the middle of the glade.

Chest heaving from her dash away from the castle, she sat back on her heels and inhaled the pine-scented air. Today it might take more than her favorite hideaway to restore her peace.

She dried her tears with the edge of the Gunn clan's woolen plaid draped around her slight frame, then studied her surroundings.

Ears keen to a rustling in the nearby underbrush, her breath caught in her throat. Her heart pounded as the peace around her shattered.

A flash of red through the branches confirmed her worst fears moments before Devlin, the captain of Isla's personal guard pushed through the undergrowth into the clearing. The laird's wife insisted on the unique shirt color as proof of their authority, except it only made the ruffians easier to spot...and avoid.

Until today.

"Look who I found outside the castle gates." Devlin sneered from a stone's toss away. "Thought ye could sneak out, did ye?"

Mayhap there was naught to fear but another tongue-lashing. Still, Moira slowly eased to her feet, prepared to bluff her way out of the danger prickling the back of her neck.

Either that or run.

Except even with scattered thickets and patches of brambles, the stretch of forest between the castle wall and the nearby ravine wouldna hide her for long.

Devlin took a step closer. "Lady Isla sent ye to the kitchens for a reason."

'Twas punishment for ruining her gown as they broke their fast that morn, except 'twasna her fault. Ilsa's spoiled son Roan had smeared the fruit tart onto her skirt, then stood silently by—and smirking—whilst Moira shouldered the blame.

"But I didna..." Her voice trailed off. Her father's new wife never believed her and lately she'd spent more time away from her family than with them.

"Ye were sent to prepare the meal for yer clan." Devlin crossed bulging arms across his chest, an angry scowl marring his face.

Moira side-stepped a patch of multi-colored flowers to put more distance between them.

She might have been happy helping in the kitchens, but the cook had complained she was underfoot and didna belong there.

Didna seem she belonged anywhere.

Especially by her father's side.

A sob caught in her throat. The whole clan had been abuzz for days with speculation about their laird's mysterious illness until she simply couldn't face another moment of the gossip feeding her fears.

What would she do if he died? Who would protect her then?

Members of their clan came to offer their herbal cures and pay their respects to their laird. Yet she wasna even allowed to sing for him like she had many times before.

Still, a lass should be allowed to greet her father on her birthday, especially her thirteenth when she officially moved from bairn to maiden.

She fingered the jeweled brooch hanging from a leather cord around her neck. Her gift three years ago while her mother was still alive.

Today held no gifts, only a heavy cloud.

The verra reason she'd sought the neglected side gate in the curtain wall and slipped away to rail at the injustice her life had become.

When Father Tomas returned from the Sinclair holding, she would ask him why good people died. And why God seemed so far away.

A twig snapped.

Too late, Moira realized she'd gotten distracted by her musings.

In three quick steps, Devlin reached her side and a hand snaked out to wrap around the plaited hair hanging down her back.

"Don't ya ken? It be dangerous for a lass to be alone in the woods."

Panic coursed through her veins and she struggled against the tightening grip that anchored her in place. "Let me go. My da will hear of this and—"

"He won't be causing any more trouble. And neither will ye." He laughed, his foul breath hot on her face. "And ye won't be needin' this anymore." A vicious jerk later and her precious heirloom had been ripped away.

The burning fire around her throat mirrored the agonizing void in her heart. "My mother's brooch—"

"Not anymore."

A moment later, he waved his dagger before her eyes.

Icy dread settled in her stomach at the sight of the wickedly sharp blade.

"There's only room for one pretty lady at the keep."

"I'm just a lass." She struggled to break free of his hold.

Was he here out of some sort of misguided loyalty? Or jealousy on behalf of his mistress?

Heaven help her if he meant to scar her for life.

A brutal yank on her hair sent her spinning. He released her for an instant, but before she could gather her wits, she found herself facing the clearing but trapped against his body. Anchored in place by a meaty hand on her forehead.

"Yer the one he's calling for in his fevered sleep." His dagger danced before her eyes. "All he can say is 'Mor.' "

Her heard ached at the drawn-out—cruel—imitation of a suffering man's delirium. Then stopped as recognition dawned.

"Mor. Mor." The traitorous guard's mocking laughter rang out through the clearing as cold metal trailed down her cheek.

Moira's knees weakened at the sound of her dear mother's name. The mother who'd died in childbirth followed a few days later by her infant son. Would they all soon be reunited in the hereafter?

"Well, no more." The blade came to rest beneath her chin.

Lightheaded with fear, her knees buckled and she found herself falling, slipping from his grasp even as the prick of the blade pierced her neck, then sliced up the side of her face with agonizing heat.

Her scream was silenced by harsh reality. With the knife at her throat, he had truly meant to kill her.

Only God could help her now.

A surge of unexpected strength sent her rolling to her right, then scrambling to her feet before running blindly into the woods. The crashing of feet behind her drove her further from the safety of home and toward the distant rush of water as she darted one way and then the other around trees.

Despite the hand pressed against her face, every step jarred the injury, sending more blood trickling through her fingers and down her arm.

She rounded a cluster of tall bushes, then glanced back over her shoulder. He gained on her, a look of fury twisting his features and the bloody dagger still in his hand.

Suddenly, the ground fell away, leaving her to tumble down the rock-strewn wall of the ravine. After a final rolling catapult off a large boulder, she landed on her back near the creek. Gasping like a fish on land, she fought to draw air into her lungs.

Above her came a bellow of outrage, reminding her to stay quiet—and motionless—in case he couldn't already see her broken body at the bottom of the ravine.

A moment later, the vice-like grip around her chest eased enough for her to breathe again. Just in time for every bruise and scrape acquired during her fall to raise their voices in protest, joining the pulsing agony from her face.

Risking detection as Devlin stomped overhead, she lifted weak hands to hold the slashed flesh together, then bit back a whimper at the renewed throbbing that brought tears to her eyes.

"When I find ye, ye'll wish ye were already dead."

Death might be welcome considering the misery of the moment. Then again, her father had always told her to be a brave lass because Gunns never quit.

A deep growl in the brush above her 'twas followed by a howl that sent chills up her already-battered spine. A wolf. Somehow, either the man's actions or the scent of her blood had attracted the attention of the beast.

The guard's war cry split through the air and soon the sounds of battle between man and beast faded further away.

Thank Heaven for the distraction, but the rest of the pack might be nearby.

Still dizzy from her fall, Moira eyed a nearby cluster of purple-hued bell heather. A half hour past, she would have relished the simple beauty of the flowering blooms and soaked in the happy twittering of lapwings in the branches overhead.

Yet now, she could already tell her body weakened from the loss of blood. If she didna wish to die when Devlin returned, she must get away.

Now.

Somehow, she staggered to her feet and stumbled along the creek bed toward the loch.

Her last memory was of coming upon an elderly man with a wooden cart.

ABOUT THE AUTHOR

Candee Fick is a romance editor for a small Christian press and a multi-published award-winning author. She is the wife of a high school football coach and the mother of three children, including a daughter with a rare genetic syndrome. When not busy editing or writing, she can be found cheering on the home team at sporting events, exploring the great Colorado outdoors, indulging in dark chocolate, and savoring happily-ever-after endings through a good book.

In addition to writing clean faith-based romance novels and inspirational non-fiction, Candee coaches other authors with their marketing plans and offers content editing to aspiring novelists. She is a member of both American Christian Fiction Writers (ACFW) and the Christian Proofreaders and Editors Network. Her fiction has semi-finaled, finaled, and won the ACFW Genesis Contest and Selah Awards.

Visit her website: https://CandeeFick.com

www.ingramcontent.com/pod-product-compliance
Lightning Source LLC
Chambersburg PA
CBHW030541130626
46552CB00006B/2371